Dangerous Suggestions

Tales & Stories

Steve Levin

The Amazon Endure typeface was designed by 2K/DENMARK in 2025.
Template id: ST-414D415A-25-A01
Printed in The United States.
E-Pub ISBN: 979-8-9996049-0-3
Hardcover ISBN: 979-8-9996049-2-7
Paperback ISBN: 979-8-9996049-1-0

DEDICATION

For Chris, obviously

"We have of the universe only formless, fragmentary visions, which we complete by the association of arbitrary ideas, creative of dangerous suggestions."

Marcel Proust
The Fugitive

CONTENTS

AUTHOR'S PREFACE

I don't remember when I first knew I wanted to write. I suspect it was while I was in high school, maybe not long after I had decided to become a doctor. There was certainly a time in my teen years when I believed I would both practice medicine and write. When I began my college studies at Duke, admission to medical school was incredibly competitive and I realized early on that if I wanted to go into medicine it was necessary to excel in my pre-med studies, and I did. Still, I didn't let go of my writing dream. I reasoned that I could come back to writing later in life, but that going to medical school right after college was my only opportunity to become a physician.

In the spring semester of my junior year I took a course in Proust taught by Wallace Fowlie. Dr. Fowlie was an engaging, enthusiastic teacher and I was mesmerized by *Remembrance of Things Past*. Every night I would end my studies parked in a club chair with my feet resting on an ottoman in Perkins library. I would lose myself in Proust's salons and the French countryside for an hour or two. By semester's end, with Proust as my inspiration, I was determined to write a novel. I spent that summer in New Orleans with Chris. She worked as a waitress on the breakfast and lunch shift at the Holiday Inn in the French Quarter. I worked from noon to 8:00 as a play therapist at a psychiatric hospital near Tulane. Our conflicting schedules left us little time together, but I did have plenty of time to write in the mornings. My novel was a coming of age story that was a barely disguised retelling of the summer of 1972. That summer, after my freshman year in college, I lived at home and worked as a construction laborer. My best friend Bruce was a bus boy at Shoney's. We spent our evenings playing tennis, smoking weed and drinking. We each had disastrous love affairs that spiraled into depression when they fell apart as the summer ended. In the background there was Watergate, the quixotic McGovern campaign, our growing friendship and much more. It was all I knew to write about but that was plenty.

When I returned to school for my senior year I gave Dr. Fowlie a small

1

selection of what I had written. He was enthusiastic about it, but I realized that other than the few pages I had shared, I had nothing else worthy to show him. The rest was rambling, aimless and a torture to read. I did not abandon the project, but I did set it aside to prepare for medical school.

While I had been diligent in college and spent many hours studying, it was nothing compared to what was required for medical school. Classes began at 8:00 every morning and other than breaks for meals I was studying until 11:00 at night. I gave no thought to working on the novel, although when I reached my clinical rotations in the third and fourth years, my creative drive burst through in the writing of a few poems. It was during those clinical rotations that I came to confront the faces of suffering and death that had previously been an abstraction to me. In this writing I expressed my struggle to understand how to live with these dark realities.

West Hospital, Fifteenth Floor, South Wing

As Mama lies on West 15
Each dusk they bring themselves
To celebrate the siege together.
With dark their faces reassume
A televised reflected pallor.
Mama's paleness flickers.
Tonsured as an old Franciscan,
The voids inside her hollow chest
Consume her.
Even the blind could see she has....

Gowned in green and white
I carry smart sophistication
And hone the ear
To gauge the feeble breaths
Marking the countdown to the end
Of pain.

Her aging husband scurries
Like nurses won't or can't
Fetching his beloved Pearl
Ice, and soothing juices.
Her young son sits hunched frozen still,
With old dog eyes,
Old sad man eyes,
Aglow from almost crying.
Her daughter wore no bra
(Who could not help but notice?)
And standing arms-crossed, angry,
Scared,
Scowls haughty at men
In green and white.

Mama moans.
Her agonies echo in my skull.
Old nurse, obey my call
For vials of hot yellow,
A distraction for the bold Crab's claw,

And morphine.

So soon I will arise
And finally say "Goodnight,"
To briefly sleep, my one retreat,
Dreamlessly;
Or if the stars should be aligned
From darkened vision may spring light
A soft cheeked daughter
In the cold of night.
But not Mama.
Mama's dead.
Unleashed, the battered souls give way
To one more vacant bed
On West 15.

General Medicine ICU: Christmas, 1978

Gray is the color of this sad town.
From township walls
To hospital halls,
Lee rides proud, no shroud:
Determined.

Does the old man dream,
Tangled in his plastic tubing,
Wired to a TV screen?
The air's alive with nurses
Humming back to Donna Summer.
Shaking hips.

Where did you go?

Your eyes aren't shut,
Reflect no light.
Mouth taped and tubed for life's last lines:
No moans.
And naked there
They smirked.
Die. Please Willie, die.
This protest is for the living
And you are no more among us.
Let these gray mean halls release
Your faded gentle wife.
She once could set you free so softly.

How I ache each time I touch you.
What was Willie once before these empty days?
God's grace   I do not know.
Creating inhumanity,

Falsely,
Fleetingly.
Old death cares not
For such graces well outside her province.
No lovely scenes requires she,
But even painless ugly,
Kicks the heart and burns the eyes.

One can only sigh and wonder:
One day to lie alone.

And then this last one, written as I was approaching medical school graduation.

An Invocation

Dark
Away through branching steel,
No neon mercy on my shoulder,
This late night lost
And aching.
Pasted crescent light
On old Church Hill
Missed its mark
But carried,
Carried down deep circles,
Carried down where cold is ever colder,
And gathered older darkness,
The crumbling brick and mortar,
And surrounding as a cap and shroud,
And shivering:
I am leaving.

The air is thick on old Church Hill,
A creeping mist invoked from unleashed wine.
Tired,
Sighing,
Heavy in small warmth,
Her living aches unwrapped, set free,
Thighs quiver smooth as ivory.
And yet she will not know the night.
(The last one?...Tomorrow?)
Still, each one matters,
All these stars,
All these seeds of indiscretion.

Time sweeps undimmed.
A quiet soft as wet as silk.
An unrelenting scream.

Under the steaming spotlight
In the late night lonely nursery,
The paper wall zoo breathes smoke,
Blows fire.
From above fall life lines plastic,
Lines curling as a pig's tail
Pasted to a baby's belly.
In a crackback seizure
Eyes roll white,
Hands grapple wild with furies unknown,
Unknowing.
I call for Valium,
Sweet potion of emotion.
Oh, may the tides be with you now,
Good Doctor,
Kind Doctor.

Counsel me,
Who held Moriah's glistening sword.
Hear this voice,
Wailing in the darkening hour,
Knees in the dust at Neilah's gate.
A thoughtless surmise,
An undeserved sleep,
A ferry for the child,
Unblemished vessel of a whispered dream,
To hopeless silence.
Send courage swift and straight,
The grace of love that I might wake.
Such fusion in this burdened soul,
Most kind caress--
Time's peace.

For is this heart unchanged,
And sad unchanging.
Awed
And numbed,
Forgive me now--
This night is near--
And soon I will be leaving.

Good Doctor,
Kind Doctor,
In pale starry dawn on old Church Hill
The demons hide,
The shadows glide together.
Ears tuned,
I tiptoe soft,
Unheard.

After medical school I moved to Philadelphia for my pediatric residency where I worked long hours in a high stress environment. Whereas in medical school I was a student watching others take care of patients, now I was the doctor and those decisions were mine to make. Most of my supervision came from residents who were only a year or two more experienced than I was. In my eyes those residents were like Greek gods. They were very powerful and very flawed. Some would later serve as models for characters in the stories I would write.

In June, 1982 I completed my residency. My first job was with the National Health Service Corps and my assignment was a practice in Camden, NJ, just across the river from Philadelphia. Not long after beginning there, my boss asked me to take over a satellite office in south Camden. The doctor working there was preparing to retire and they wanted me to replace him. I was happy to accept the post. The office was small and rather quiet. During a typical day I might see ten to fifteen patients, about half the workload of a normal pediatric practice. With all that free time, I began to read fiction again, and when I grasped I was going to have many very slow days, I began once more to read Proust. Once again, Proust inspired me to write. Just then, one of the other pediatricians announced she was pregnant and planned to return to work part time after her baby arrived. I asked my boss if she and I could share a job so I could work part time as well, and he agreed.

So, at summer's end in 1984 I reduced my hours practicing medicine to two days a week. I spent the other days toiling over a novel in my third floor study. This was not the same book I had begun in college. This was a story of a wise cracking bartender who attempts to locate and retrieve a stolen Vermeer. There were songs and dreams, flashbacks and fantasies. I was reading a lot of Pynchon then.

After a few months of throwing all of my energy into this project, I realized I had no idea what I was doing. I knew I no longer wanted to write this novel, but I still wanted to write. I began to write short fiction, and I also came to understand that writing is not intuitive. It is a craft that one must study. I took creative writing classes at Penn. I joined a writer's group in West Philadelphia where we would meet once a month to critique each other's work. I enjoyed all of this, and my writing improved.

The pieces in this collection were all created between 1985 and 1988. I was proud of them, but by the end, I had come to appreciate that I was a better physician than I was a writer. (And you may possibly think "I would hope so"

9

after you finish your reading.) I also understood that my strong desire to play whatever small role I could to make this world a better place could best be achieved by practicing medicine. The final omen that it was time to put my writing dreams aside occurred not long after my story, "A Private Investigation," was accepted by a small magazine for publication. Just as we were ready to go to press, the magazine went out of business. It was definitely time to turn the page, as it were, on this writing adventure. By then I was also the father of a two-year-old and we were planning to have more children. So yeah, money was a consideration, too. I put my stories in a file cabinet, stored them on a rarely used hard drive, and I didn't look at them again for many years.

During the pandemic my great friend Bruce approached me with an idea. He wanted to take our letters and create a book out of them. He and I had written to each other extensively during college. The correspondence had dwindled considerably afterwards, but then in the mid-nineties we picked up again and wrote letters to each other roughly once a month for almost ten years. Unfortunately, we then joined the twenty first century and stayed in touch by text, phone and email. In February 2025, we published the second edition of his work, *As Always: The Letters of Pickles and Zorro*. Bruce had done an amazing job of assembling our correspondence of 265 letters and of filling in narrative to explain the gaps and inside jokes. I had followed on in this second edition with my own comments, additions and pictures.

Reading this volume of letters lifted me. My letters were good. They weren't Proust, but they were funny, they were serious, and on occasion they were eloquent. I had forgotten how well I could write. As I read those letters I was startled to see that the story I wanted to tell when I had begun writing long ago in New Orleans was right there in front of me. To be sure, it wasn't a novel, but this work conveyed the passions and the friendship that was the heart of that long ago abandoned attempt.

And so, having retired from medicine and with my children now grown, I rummaged through the back of my file cabinet and pulled out the stories. The hard drive was so old it wouldn't connect to any modern computer. I read the stories and found myself attending an unexpectedly happy reunion with long forgotten companions. I began to work on the best of them again. A few needed serious editing, while others just required a few additions or deletions. Now, I give them to you. Some are simply tales and nothing more. The best are stories that provoke, answering some questions but leaving an ambiguity for you to ponder.

As you read the stories keep in mind the times when they were written. In 1985, there were no cell phones, no internet and a gallon of gas cost $1.12. "Guerilla Love" grew out of a paranoid fantasy when my house had a rapid and unfortunate sequence of plumbing failures. "Night Shift Legends" and "Crossing the Line" were inspired by the lives of those senior residents I mentioned. I was immersed in Tolstoy, Dostoyevsky, and Pushkin when I wrote "Registration," "The Duel" and probably "Forget it, Jake." Today, I don't believe I could have written "You and RubyBlades." I would be accused of cultural appropriation and reducing my characters to stereotypes. I plead guilty. Throughout my many years of practicing medicine I was immersed in Black culture. It was not unusual for me to spend an entire day at work and not encounter another Caucasian. I learned that there are elements of Black experience that I could never fully penetrate. I accept that and would never pretend otherwise. At the same time, there are universal human traits that we share. Both of these conditions can be true. So yes, some of these characters are stereotypes, but RubyBlades and Ink are completed children. Their story is genuine, their friendship is real, and their brief adventure has a wonderful momentum. Their story is one of my favorites.

Take what you will from this slim volume. For me, it's been a great joy to journey back to another time in my life and visit again with these old friends.

A PRIVATE INVESTIGATION

"Is it true what they say about you?" That's the first thing she asks when we're alone in the library, so already I have my doubts. It's a genuine rich man's library where the volumes crowding the varnished oak bookcases are all dust-covered, crack-spined, hardbacks. I'm standing behind the bar (look, if they want to put a bar in the library, who am I to complain?), poised like Cary Grant pouring two gin and tonics. My uncle, our host, has even left freshly cut lime slices in a fluted crystal bowl, and still she has to ask, "Is it true what they say about you?"

Barefoot and dressed in swimming trunks I pad across the hardwood floor, but if my costume were a smoking jacket of the finest silk brocade I would emanate the same debonair assurance. After all, I have answered this same question, in one form or another, many times in my twenty-nine years. She graciously accepts the drink, and I thrust my head oddly forward so that my nostrils just kiss the creamy nape of her neck. I sniff. Loose wisps of sandy blonde hair grace my cheek; and though we've hardly met, I'm falling in love. Surprised, but confident, I murmur, "Chanel Number 5, 1983."

Lucy steps back and looks at me curiously. At twenty two she's so young, so fair-skinned and fresh, that even though her Chanel tells me otherwise, I still hope she is the writer. Her indigo bathing suit must be new, for where the straps scoop low there is a forbidding untanned arc scalloped across her full upper breasts. The sheeny Gottex suit clings to descending ribs, to her flat belly, and rises high over flawlessly carved hips. She pushes back the damp ends of hair resting on her shoulder and shrugs regally. "Very impressive."

"You sound surprised. I guess none of your college boys have that kind of skill. Don't think it stops there."

"I hadn't heard there was more." She arches her eyebrows, watching me as she sips the bitter drink. Her blue eyes sparkle and tease.

"Play your cards right and you just might find out."

"In the library?" It sounds like a dare, but why is she wearing Chanel?

"Why not?" I ask.

"Shame on you, Lance," she squeals in delight. "In your Uncle's library."

To hell with Chanel. I step closer and set my drink on the credenza. Let Aunt Theresa worry about the water ring. "They're all fussing over the happy couple. No one's looking for us." I rub my fingertips gently along her shoulders and faintly sing, "Oh, let us go sin, you and I."

But she pretends I'm joking and draws away laughing. "Tell me about it."

"My special talent?" I ask, knowing this is exactly what she means.

"Yeah, that magic sense of smell."

I take a deep breath. "There isn't much to say. For some reason, the only thing I can smell is perfume. I don't know why, but that's the extent of my olfactory capability."

"You really can't smell anything else?" She sounds so incredulous I wonder what she expected.

"Listen, that's an improvement. Until I was sixteen I couldn't smell anything at all."

"I don't believe this. Who told you when I bought it?"

"Yes. Well, that's the other part. I know it sounds strange, but I'm so sensitive to perfumes I can also tell the year a scent was bottled. I'll grant you, year to year differences are rather slight. Still, they are detectable."

"Did Jenny put you up to this?" she asks; then she asserts, "She put you up to this. Oh, it must have been Jenny. It sounds just like her. She showed you my bottle of Chanel, didn't she?"

The last of my hopes fades to a glimmer. "No. Jenny's too busy planning her wedding. Go ahead. Try me. Jean Nate, Opium, Decadence, Giorgio. I know all of them, and hundreds more. Go ahead, and I'll tell you their vintages as well. Seriously, perfume has a vintage, just like wine. Well, maybe it's not like wine. How would I know? I've never smelt wine."

She's the most beautiful girl I've ever spoken to, and once again I'm the circus freak banished to his tent somewhere along the midway between the fire-eater and the two-headed ram. I realize now I've pinched the wrong suspect, but she's so lovely I hate to let her go. I lower my eyes and tell her, "You know, as afflictions go, mine isn't too bad."

Suddenly, the library door bursts open. A young man with the shoulders of a bull, the chest of a fighter, and the curly locks and face of Adonis trumpets impatiently, "Lucy, I've been looking all over for you. They're waiting for us on the boat." He doesn't even glance at me. Lucy trots obediently to the door and

13

is almost out before she turns and says, "Thanks for the drink."

Oh yes, as afflictions go mine isn't too bad. What am I but this year's parlor game, a mild amusement for the idle curious when the possibilities of Charades, Trivial Pursuit, and even Risk have been exhausted?

I take the letter out of my shirt pocket and look at it again:

Dearest Lance,

Does time rob us of more than our memories? Is there no hope? But who, you ask, and how? Come to your uncle's on Saturday. Once there, you will certainly know how to find me.

All my love,

This strange, unsigned letter came in the mail two days ago. Well, it's not exactly unsigned, because it reeks of perfume: L'air du Temps, 1977. It's an unusual scent; I haven't sniffed it in years. And she knew it. Of course she knew it, and she also knew that without her letter I would have declined my uncle's invitation. Despite my best efforts, I find nothing but despair at these gatherings. Everyone here seems so smoothly impenetrable, so superficial, and it's no secret there's no escape once you arrive at these parties. But how could I discard such a promise? So here I am, this scent my only clue.

Oh, if it had only been the beautiful young Lucy.

I tuck the letter away and leave the airconditioned library for the soggy heat of the afternoon. The large wooden deck I step upon overlooks a yard that gently slopes down to the water, a crooked riverbank once wild and brown but now coaxed green. Its rows of hedges are neatly trimmed. While above the sun has floated and now falls across the sky, I deliberate on where to renew my search. I could enlist the aid of the gentlemen carousing with my uncle's business partner beneath the shady maples. (For as Raymond Chandler says, "The pursuit of knowledge, brother, is the asking of questions.") Or I could descend the finely manicured lawn, for I know most of the ladies by the pier. They are old acquaintances from my high school days. Like lizards harassed by the heat, they lie sprawled upon chaise lounges underneath a huge umbrella. What a crushing disappointment it would be to learn that one of them is my unknown author. I decide the ice cubes in my glass look lonely and head for the bar.

The bar is a make-shift affair: at one end of the deck, three card tables have been pushed together and covered with a long white table cloth. Sea-green and amber bottles stand perched solemnly on either side, and chests of crushed ice peek from underneath the white skirt. As is my custom at these affairs, I have been a frequent visitor to the bar, and I feel a certain empathy for the bartender, an older, heavy-set Black man who is dressed quite formally for this informal party: stiff white coat over starched white shirt. His collar is thoroughly drenched in sweat. I converse with him whenever I go over for another drink, for I think he might appreciate the friendly banter. But each time I walk over with my empty glass and anticipation of recognition, he looks me in the face, but not the eyes, and with an easy grin he asks, "And what'll it be, Sir?"

"One singing mermaid on the rocks."

"Pardon?"

"Another gin and tonic."

"Lance, my boy, come on over here." My uncle's business partner is shouting up to me. "How's it going fella? Looks like you've lost a few pounds." In my swimming trunks I look quite thin. I'm also losing my hair. I climb down the steps, scoot around a wooden tub of geraniums and approach him.

"A donation to the Ethiopian relief fund," I tell him, amazed once more he's made his fortune selling clothes. Today, he is dressed in the standard uniform for these occasions: snappy green, purple and gold mingle like boorish guests in the plaid of his stiff Bermuda shorts. A burnt-orange Lacoste shirt clings to his bloated chest and belly.

"Oh, I like that. A donation to the Ethiopian relief fund." His large mouth stretches like putty, and he pats his waist. "I should give some too. So how's that research coming?"

"It's slow," I tell him. "You wouldn't believe the obstacles when you're so close to the project. It wrecks havoc with every concept of experimental design. But what can I do? The work is really fascinating, and there's always the possibility of meeting interesting people. And at least the people at Revlon are happy." The people at Revlon have recruited me for a special investigation, though I have no idea how they found out about my unusual abilities. Perhaps the government keeps a registry somewhere. With virgin teenage males as my subjects (I won't talk about how difficult *they* are to find), I'm searching for any possible correlations that may exist between the well known—and wonderful— physical changes of puberty and certain selective changes in the olfactory pathways.

He says, "Now listen, son, as soon as you hit on something big, you make sure you let me know. No reason we can't all cash in on that special beak of yours. Until then," he chuckles, "just keep that nose to the grindstone." He laughs again at his joke, then adds, "I mean it. There's something in this for both of us."

"Lance, if you really want to do something worthwhile, figure out a way to stop the Devils," says another cousin, a furrier from Baltimore whom no one has seen for ten years. "They never lose."

"What?"

"The basketball team," my uncle's partner enlightens me. He turns to the furrier, "I keep telling you, you've got to drop a man from the weak side into the middle. If you don't, they'll flip the ball inside, and it's two points for sure."

"And leave Rutstein open on the wing? No way. You can't do it. You can't afford to leave that guy open."

"Rutstein, Rutstein. That's all anyone talks about. Rutstein." The businessman flaps his pudgy arms. Although I'm not a fan I've heard about this fellow Rutstein. Who hasn't? He's a short, bearded fellow who can jump sixty inches off the floor and has the fastest hands since Harry Houdini. As with all outrageous phenomena, he has engendered a crisis among the paranoid: they are uncertain if he heralds an ascendancy or an abdication. The level-headed simply assume he's a quirk of nature. You can understand why I feel a certain kinship with the man.

The partner chatters on, "Listen, Mr. Big Shot Fur Salesman, if you really want to make some money, stop betting against the Devils and sell a mink or two to that lady over there." He points to a white colonial mansion that strides the crest of the opposite shore. "She could buy your whole inventory and still have closet space for mine. Mo-ney." His tongue hangs on the word. A gardener astride a lawnmower crisscrosses her neatly kept grounds. On one side the towering mansion is flanked by a pair of tennis courts, while on the other a redwood fence encircles what is probably a swimming pool.

"Who lives there?" I ask.

"Mrs. Joe Pudley. As in Pudley Pickles. Poor guy keeled over three months ago with a heart attack. Fifty-five years old, but those pickles could be peanuts for all the good they do him now. Hey, that's life, right Lance?"

A sudden blast of music pierces the quiet afternoon. Chirping sparrows skitter across the river at the sound of an old Doors' song. Jim Morrison maliciously croons:

I'm a spy
In the house of love.
I know the dream
That you're dreaming of.

Not one to miss a chance to retreat when I see it, I tell them, "I better get to that tape player before Uncle David smashes it. See you gents later." But old habits being what they are, instead of heading straight for the music, I return to the bar. I can't decide if I should ask the bartender what he thinks of Rutstein or repeat my mermaid joke. I compromise and simply ask for a refill of my gin and tonic.

In the later afternoon, as the furious heat of this June day wanes, the guests, like creatures of the desert at night, slowly gather in the expansive open yard. Some emerge from the shadows of the shade trees, while others arise from the cool green river. The women though still linger near the pier, their laughter ringing between sips of strawberry daiquiris.

When I leave the bar I see the motorboat carrying Lucy and her friends approach from up the river. Beautiful Lucy's long hair trails behind her in the breeze. Is she returning to me? She laughs and clutches my cousin Jennifer, the future bride. In the wake of the droning motorboat skis the tanned Adonis. Balanced perfectly on one waterski, he skims over the ripples straight for the shore, and just as it seems inevitable that he must smash into my uncle's pier, he swiftly cuts back, shooting off a rainbow spray of river water that topples the trio soaking in the floating lounge chairs. They screech and curse Adonis before they climb back into their chairs. My uncle is very proud of those floating lounges: he has waterproofed them so they cannot rust, put styrofoam pads on the arm rests and foot supports so they cannot sink, and now like corks those chairs bob in the river. I'm sure he's relieved Adonis hasn't destroyed them.

After the boat passes the music booms louder, so I circle around to the side of the house. Packed tightly together, a row of rhododendrons lines the wall of this modern ranch-style home. Hidden among these bushes lurk two couples, friends of the betrothed. A blaring cassette deck announces their spot of concealment. When I climb inside the bushes, I see they are passing a joint. Of course I cannot smell it, and perhaps it is the slick-green of rhododendron leaves or the angle of the sun, but the curls of rising smoke seem yellow. Roger shakes his head when I decline the offered hit. He croaks without exhaling,

"It's good stuff, man."

"Columbian?" I ask. I want to make it clear I know the lingo even if I don't participate. Shari and Jerri, the two girls, whisper and giggle behind another branch. Always on the lookout, I decide to get a whiff of them. I push aside the branch between us, but when I squeeze through the foliage, I trip over a root, stagger into both girls, and just as we all tumble into the bushes, a branch slingshots behind me whacking Roger across the mouth. He howls in pain. My face is buried in Jerri's navel. I find this hot flesh on flesh delectable, but the girls quickly scramble from beneath me.

"Sorry," I mumble sincerely when we're all standing again. I try to brush some crusty leaves off Shari's leg, but she pushes my hand away. It doesn't matter: she's wearing some Estee Lauder trash and Jerri nothing—no perfume, that is—at all.

Roger rubs his cheek as he squats down to search for the joint. "Hey Lance, keep cool. No need to tell the world we're here."

Jerri titters, "Hey world, we're smoking reefer under the trees."

Shari chimes in, "Let's put up a neon sign. You know, a bitching blinking arrow that says, 'DRUGS, THIS WAY!!!'"

I retrieve my glass. "You guys ought to cut down the music or David'll come stomping back here with State Cops and blood hounds. He hates drugs."

Roger picks up the joint and draws three quick puffs to ignite the ash. "No. Davie's cool. He knows everybody smokes. Sure you don't want some?"

"No thanks. The few times I tried it, I only got sleepy. I prefer another poison." I answer, displaying my glass.

Shari says, "You better stay away from poison. You know what happened to old Joe Pudley."

"I heard he had a heart attack."

"No way," Roger insists. "His old lady slipped him something sketchy, and now the bitch is living high on the hog."

Nudging my elbow, Jerri says in a husky voice, "Come on, Lance. Loosen up. Take a toke and join the twenty-first century. Wake up and smell the coffee." For some reason Shari finds this hilariously funny. She falls to her knees clutching her stomach. Tears of glee roll down her cheeks.

"Smell the coffee," she gasps, kneeling in the dirt.

Irritated, I hack my way through the branches. I'm almost free of the rhododendrons when Nelson, who's been as solemn as a monument since I joined them, grabs my arm. The force of his grip surprises me. Exploding blood vessels radiate from the sunsets in his heavy-lidded eyes. "Lance," he tells me earnestly, "He lives. Morrison lives."

I have to think for a minute before I understand. "Nelson, how can I break this to you gently? Jim Morrison died years ago in Paris." A straddled branch thrusts rudely into my crotch. I raise myself onto tiptoes, but Nelson is too enraptured to notice my discomfort.

"No, that's what they want you to believe. But check out the facts—no one ever saw the body. He lives, Lance. People have seen him. He has returned to tell. He has returned to tell us all."

I pry myself free of his grasp, and as I emerge from the rhododendrons I call back to him, "Nelson, if he has something interesting to say, let me know."

I wipe the dirt from my knees, straighten my trunks, but my ears still sting from Shari's laughter. Like everyone else, I want to join the party, but I must also sort for clues among what is here and what is missing. I have mentioned my research: I seek explanations at the source of change. I know more about the sense of smell than any person who smells would care. So where does that lead me? How am I supposed to know? I can only smell perfume.

In the shimmering twilight between sunset and darkness, thick-dropped dew clings to the soft blades of grass. The river breeze is cooler now. Some of the guests have departed, but the ladies smeared in oil still cackle beneath the umbrella. My grumbling conscious reminds me I've avoided their perfumes, but my reluctance persists. I've known these women since my childhood, and it seems we have never understood the same language. Why would one of them suddenly desire me now? And even if one did, I cannot imagine loving her; for these women are wizened and cynical, devoid of possibilities, though none of them are even thirty. How could love flourish in such weary plains? I look at them, all flabby shanks and bangled earrings, and wonder if I would rather remain ignorant than confront such disappointment.

On the other hand, I have endured this afternoon, and I know my search is incomplete if I fail to explore this one last lead. I quickly down a double gin and tonic to brace myself. Go on, Lance. Go meet the disappointing truth.

Stretched out on her back Tigre peers at me through her oversized sunglasses. "Well, if it isn't the Wizard of Schnozz. What do you think of these upcoming nuptials?"

The four women are fanned out around me. Distracted by a menagerie of scents, I mumble, "Oh, I don't know. I hope it works out."

Obsession says, "I don't give it much hope." She squints at the remaining guests. "I would guess at least half the men here have slept with the bride. Excluding most of her relatives, of course."

"And half of them don't expect marriage to change that," retorts Cachet.

"Me neither," Wind Song agrees.

Tigre asks, "I wonder how she explained her scar to him? You know, the one from her 'infection.'"

"Oh, you know Jennifer," laughs Cachet. "She probably told him it was her appendix. At least she still has one good tube."

"Thanks a million. How about getting me another drink?"

"We have a wonderful relationship," Cachet explains to me. "She calls the shots and I pour them." She turns back to Tigre, "You don't need a friend. You need a maid."

"Like young widow Pudley," chimes in Obsession. "Jacki says she's wearing only red and black this year. Nothing else, just red and black."

To which Tigre, curling her lip, responds, "Marvelous. Now I'll have to buy a whole new wardrobe."

I would prefer she buy a new perfume, but I say, "Who is this Pudley woman? People have been talking about her all afternoon." I look over the darkening river at her mansion.

Wind Song raises her eyes from her fingernails. "Oh Lance, you're so simple sometimes. We all went to school with her. It's Colleen Zitwer."

"Colleen Zitwer," I cry. Her name resonates in the corridors of my past. For as I said, it wasn't until adolescence that I began to smell perfume, and this is what transpired on that most miraculous day. I was studying math, geometry if you really want to know, when this same Colleen Zitwer burst late into class, huffing out of breath and smelling of Shalimar. I was startled. Triangles took on new meanings. Shy though I was, I asked her out. And she accepted. Once we went to a dance, a wondrous sockhop in our high school gymnasium. I remember streamers floating across the ceiling, bleachers shoved against the wall and stacked with coats. I still treasure the glorious memory of Colleen pressed tightly to me, her head snug upon my shoulder, as we whirled across the varnished floor. The band, sneaking whiskey from a paper sack, played miserably, but who could care? The music carried us, caressed us, my Colleen and I, through the magic of the night. A whole world sprang from her Shalimar. And then another starlit evening, undressed and uninitiated, in the back seat of my father's station wagon....Oh yes, I fell in love with her. Willingly, no greedily, I fell in love with her. Of course, she was very fond of me, and though she never shared the passion that engulfed me, she was flattered by its aura. How could I resent she never felt the same? I was too grateful for the possibilities of the universe she unveiled for me.

From Shalimar to L'air du Temps? Why not? Surely a woman can change her scent.

Or maybe that wasn't the clue at all. I reach into my pocket. "—Once there you will certainly know how to find me." She never said she would be here; and with her house in plain view, of course the guests would gossip about her. Oh, you wily Colleen.

I spy a vacant floating lounge chair and shiver with recognition: there's a vehicle for every journey. I jump upon the pier, quickly cross the wooden planks, holding tightly to the railing for my balance now is poor, and slide gingerly into the foamy dark water. Lucy and Adonis sit on the edge, but they do not look up as my chair drifts by. She has tears in her eyes as she says to him, "There are other ways to make a point without being cruel." I paddle very, very hard; and as the ever swifter current carries me away from party and pier, I can barely hear him snort before he answers, "Yes, that may be true, but none is easier."

The river is running strong, and I keep tumbling from the chair. Each time I pull myself up, I see a larger picture of her: a fashion conscious widow...a pickle heiress...who may or may not have poisoned her husband...but if she did, she did a damn good job of it. This woman hardly resembles the girl I loved, but how could she remain unchanged?

Should I then return to the party?

The middle of the river is so lovely, calm and quiet.

No. Forward, Lance, press on. Spit out the salty water. Climb back in and kick once more. Who cares if it's impossible to regain the fragrant past? You're crossing to the future. Paddle harder. After all, it's no more than half a mile across this river, and no one knows what sort of widow waits upon the other shore.

TWINS

You can't be too careful. People are always out to trick you, always looking for that easy money. Charlatans prowl the city streets and the leering smile of a grifter beckons from every doorway. Watch yourself. Beware: each scamp has baited and tossed out his own silver-tongued fishing hook. Walk down the street and you can hear the prayers for the nibble that will reel a sucker in. I would never say I'm smarter than most people, but I have wandered down a fair number of those streets. Maybe it's a question of experience. Maybe after a time your heart, as well as your head, recognizes the chant of the con man. And while that knowledge doesn't exactly make this life God's Paradise, tell me where's the joy in being somebody's fool?

I earn my money working as the chief security guard at a local hospital. On this particular day the emergency room was quiet. We'd seen a few kids screaming with earaches, and the usual fallout from a fender bender or two. One crazy Joe had been tipping the bottle while he was fixing up his Christmas tree. He had fallen off his ladder, and as he lay sprawled upon the floor he had discovered, much to his surprise, that his right arm had a joint between the wrist and elbow that his left arm didn't. When they brought him here, he was so loaded he didn't need any pain-killers. Not yet anyway. We were waiting for the plaster wrapped around his arm to dry when this wiry young man came in complaining of back pain.

"Ooh, my aching back," he moaned as he shuffled past the desk in tiny little steps. He was slightly bent at the waist, with his hands just barely touching his flanks. Even after two of the kinder aides had lifted him onto a stretcher and rolled him across the hall, he kept on blubbering until Doc Rheuss stepped over to him. I could tell the doc was irritated. He didn't even bother to shut the curtain to the room before he began questioning the man. They talked quietly for a few minutes as the doc asked about the pain; but as soon as the doc touched the sore back, the fellow let loose a horrifying, blood-curdling scream. He cried out how this torment was unbearable. He would

22

rather burn in the feverish flame than suffer from this backache, his agony was so bad.

This wailing continued while Doc Rheuss gently probed the lower back muscles. In the midst of the patient's thundering, the doc asked the man if he had any kids. At first, the man just gasped a few words between his cries of pain, but soon his groaning became softer and less urgent. When his bellowing ceased, I could hear him tell Doc Rheuss about his two daughters: the little girls' names, what schools they went to, and how the oldest one was Mary in this year's Christmas play.

The doc was still checking him, nodding his head like he was listening to every word, when he asked the man, "Do you have any pictures of them?" The fellow stretched out from the table to lift up his pants, which were lying on a chair two feet away. He drew out his wallet and twisted back around to show the doc the pictures he always carried with him. He beamed like any proud daddy would. Doc Rheuss paused. He told the patient how cute those little girls were, and then he went on with his examination. The patient moaned again, but now his whining was muffled, as if it were coming from a more distant site. When the doc had finished, he crossed his arms in front of his chest and said, "There's minimal spasm in the lumbar musculature of your back. Do you have a heating pad at home?" The man nodded. "Good, then put that on your back, right on the area that's bothering you the most, and take two extra-strength Tylenol every four hours. Get some rest. Let your wife take care of those pretty little girls. You stay off your feet for a few days, and you'll be fine in no time."

The man pointed to his back and protested, "Tylenol? Doc, you gotta be kidding. They give that shit to kids. I need something strong for this pain." I guess that young man had forgotten how easily he had twisted around to get that wallet with the pictures, but Doc Rheuss had studied every move. Like me, the old doc knows what's going on. We've seen too many folks come in here looking to get juiced up to fall for that trick. Doc Rheuss wasn't about to lose his license because some wily joker pulled the wool over his eyes. Then the man started yelling at the doctor, calling him all sorts of nasty names. At first, the doc tried to calm him down, but soon it grew clear that this fellow wasn't going to be satisfied until he had been given some kind of magic pill. So when Doc Rheuss walked out and left that patient hollering, I didn't need a genie from a lamp to figure out who had a new problem on his hands.

I'd been sipping black coffee over by the desk with Jenny, the head nurse, and we'd been listening to them. Hell, as loud as that roar was, we couldn't miss hearing them. She turned to me and said, "Ape (they call me that on account of my size), I think they need you back there."

After I drained the dregs of my coffee, I nodded to her. I hitched up my pants and ambled across to the room. As a security guard, I can't do too much if trouble starts. It's not as if I work for the police, although I do wear an officer's cap and a uniform with a badge. I rely on what you might call my presence: I'm six feet, seven inches tall, and I weigh close to three hundred pounds. The wiry man was still sitting on the stretcher with his hospital gown gaping open in the back. He was cursing when his tight face riveted its glittering, yellow eyes on me.

"What's the problem, son?"

"Damn doctor, that's the problem. My back's killing me. I got the 'Animal Spasms' and he tells me to take two goddam Tylenols. Shit. I don't have to come here for that kind of shit. Who's he think he is? Shit-brained doctor. My damn back's killing me." He was shaking his head back and forth as he rubbed his side.

"Sorry about your back, fella. I really am. But if that's what the doc says, that's what he says. I can't change that." I paused for a second. "It might be best if you just got your clothes on now and left." I always try to sound sympathetic when I start talking to people. I'll always give them the simple way out if they want to take it.

"Yeah, that's easy for you. It ain't your back biting into you every time you move. I wanna see another doctor." He was still glaring at me with those burning, hateful eyes.

I held his stare and took one step closer to the stretcher. "Like I said, I'm truly sorry about your back. But you know how it is on holidays. We've only one got doctor working here and you just saw him. Now if I were you, and I didn't like what the doctor told me, I'd head over to Riverside Hospital—it's just down the road—and see what they could do for me there. That's what I'd do. But there's nothing else we can do for you here." I nodded towards his clothes. "Why don't you get dressed? You don't seem like a man who wants to cause trouble. You know that can't help your back." I was talking quietly, talking gently. I don't let them think I'm angry and I surely don't let them think I'm scared; but I have this way of screwing up my eyes that lets them know I mean business. They always know who is in charge. The man leaned over and picked up his clothes.

"Goddam doctors don't know nothing," he muttered. I just nodded and left the room.

"Everything ok?" Jenny asked me. She looked a little anxious. The doc was already busy with another patient.

"He's putting on his clothes." Jenny was wearing a mournful smile as she shook her head, and I knew what she was thinking. You let yourself get taken too much, and there's nothing left of you. A man has got to protect his own; and with the little I have, the Lord knows I have to watch my hindside.

By the time the guy with the back pain left, my eight-hour shift had run its course. Austin, this friendly, chubby fellow who works over in patient transport, had asked me to stop by at a party that he and some other aides were giving in the employee's break room. I really wanted to go home, but I went to the party, mainly to tip my hat and say hello. I don't know why they need to have a party when they see these same people at work day after day. Do they think they'll find something new to talk about?

My footsteps echoed as I crossed the empty corridor. Never, not even in the pit of the night, had the hospital seemed such a ghost town. No laughter spilled out from the nurses' lounge. In the Heart Station, no patients sweated over the Sanskrit of their EKGs. Even cavernous Medical Records was deserted, and you could always expect to find an intern there wildly rummaging through the stacks of charts. I had just passed the emergency shower outside the Nuclear Medicine Lab when the friendly vibrations of music finally reached me from the party.

I arrived long after the celebration had commenced, but my entrance was even further delayed by a heavily tinseled Christmas tree that leaned across the doorway. Does anyone ever consider the obstacles a man of any real size must face? When I had finally squeezed inside it took me a moment to get my bearings. Austin had disconnected the overhead fluorescents and had strung holiday lights up and down the walls. The flickering green and red bulbs so greatly distorted all shapes and movements that I caught myself wondering if this was really the same room where I ate my sandwich every day. The music was far too loud for my taste, but the harsh volume didn't keep a dozen or so lab techs from dancing and laughing. You could see they were having a good time. Everyone else was fanned out around the edges, half watching the dancers, half drinking beer, half spinning tales and talking hospital gossip. Just as I grabbed a Rolling Rock, I saw Austin standing beneath a twisted crepe paper streamer across the room. He was talking with some other fellows from

25

transport that I'd seen before, but didn't know. I circled around the dancers towards them.

One of the guys I didn't know, a short and scrawny blonde haired guy with a face full of pimple craters, was talking. "Will you look at that," he said. They were watching one of the techs who was dancing with her back facing us. She was wearing a pair of black leather pants that were skin-tight. "That's something else."

Everybody nodded. Austin said to me, "Did you see that angry whore they brought in this morning?" I nodded. Earlier that day an ambulance had brought in this whore whose pimp had slashed a six inch long laceration down her back. "I couldn't believe it. That woman's lying there—furious, hurt, bleeding all over the stretcher—and she tells the cops some crazy trick went wild and sliced her up. And you know why she lies like that? You think she's trying to save herself? No way. She's trying to protect that snake 'cause she thinks he loves her. I say that man's got one weird way of showing his affections. Too much. And let me ask you this." He tapped a fat finger above my badge. "What kind of sleaze-ball pimp is going to do something like that to one of his girls? The way I figure it, the man must've been dusted. That's the only way it makes any sense. No pimp in his right mind is going to slice a girl like that—scars are bad for business. Scars are horrible for business." He shook his head with disdain at the pimp's poor judgment.

"Dusted?" I asked as I sipped my beer, my glance sliding back and forth between Austin and the dancing tech.

He laughed and slapped me on the shoulder. "Ape, where've you been, old man? Dust. Angel Dust. PCP. That stuff does wild things with your head. Makes you crazy."

"Austin, they're all crazy out there, dusted or not." I was looking at the tech wiggling out on the floor.

"You got a point there, man," he replied as he lowered his sunglasses to watch the dancer. "Ape, you got a point."

Something about the way Austin was talking about that bleeding whore started me thinking about one night last spring. It was a warm beautiful night, a night with just a whisper of a breeze. A giant full moon lit up the April sky. I was working the three to eleven shift when a wailing ambulance brought in a seven year-old girl. Her daddy had sent her to the store to buy some candy, but a truck had slammed into her as she crossed the street. She was in pretty bad shape when she arrived. Her brains were leaking out of her ears. They worked on her for a few minutes, but everyone knew from the start. When the doctor broke the news to her mother that the little girl was dead, the woman didn't believe him. She couldn't believe that her daughter had died on her way to the store to buy candy. Then she looked into the doctor's sad and serious eyes and she knew he wasn't lying to her. She knew he was telling her the truth. In her rage the woman began crying and screaming right in the middle of the emergency room. It was the worst moment of her entire life. Of all the things that had ever happened to that woman, none of them had ever been so horrible as her daughter getting killed. Her pain was real, unbelievably real, and I felt terribly sorry for the woman; but I didn't hurt. It's not that I'm a callous person. I do not believe that I am different from anybody else who sees laid bare what is usually, and best, kept hidden. But after a while, another person's pain is like his flat tire. You might help the first few strangers you pass on the highway put on a spare; but eventually, you're going to drive past somebody. I guess you have to, or you would never reach wherever you were going. So when Austin started talking that way about the angry whore and her stupid pimp, I knew what was traveling underneath his words. We're all just trying to get somewhere safe.

It was time for me to go home. I had one more beer for the road, and then I said my goodbyes. When I counted back later, I had only gulped down the two beers at the party, and a man of my size doesn't get drunk on two beers. That's not the explanation.

In the eerie winter twilight I struck out for the parking lot. As I rubbed my gloves together to warm my hands, I was thinking of hot soup, but dreaming of whiskey. The foggy low sky dropped thick pellets of sleet that rolled off my cap to weave blue streaks down my overcoat. With deliberate steps I crunched through the two day-old, mud-splattered snow that covered the sidewalk; and the menacing gray city loomed above me, goading and familiar, as I walked alone through this zone of frozen misery. I was reaching for the keys to my car when a man stepped out from the shadows into the white cone of a street light. He spoke in a quiet and respectful manner as he approached me. "Officer, I was wondering if you could help me?"

I raised an eyebrow to study the man. He was more than a few years younger than me, but he was just as big. I had no doubt he was a poor man. Under his frazzled coat he wore a hooded sweatshirt, and his soiled pants clung to legs nearly as thick as tree trunks. His wet shoes glimmered in the light; he wasn't wearing any boots. I wasn't interested in making conversation, but the

27

tone of his question caught me off guard. There was a surprising dignity in his way of asking, so I stopped and said, "Sure, son. What's the problem?" I figured his battery was dead and he needed help starting his car.

"Well," he went on, looking me straight in the face. "Three days ago my wife had twins. Everything went fine, but I just found out they're all set to go home. Sort of caught me unprepared. You see, I was sure they'd keep twins for a week. Now talk about your Christmas surprises. My car's out of gas. I got no cash to get us home since I get paid on Friday and we live pretty far away. You know where Willingboro is? We live up near there." He kept those big grey eyes fixed on mine.

I looked him over again. In the fog and the poor light, I couldn't make out his face too well, except that everything about the man seemed large. Like a turnip, his nose sprang out between the stubble on his jowls. There was nothing treacherous in his thick lipped smile, though I still checked those bulky mitts of his to see if he was carrying anything; but instead of finding a weapon when I squinted at his hands, I saw two grimy gloves with holes so big a couple of his fingers were poking through them.

I have this firm policy of not giving money to strangers. When I hear those panhandlers while I'm crossing to work, I keep my eyes straight and my money stays warm in my pocket. But I was already talking to this fellow, so I needed time to think. I said, "Sure, I know where Willingboro is. I played football in high school, and we had a few games up there."

"You played football, too?" He sounded as if it would be the most amazing coincidence that two men of our size used to play football. "I was a fullback. You know what a fullback does." He snorted a chuckle. "You get to carry the ball two times so you can block for the halfback forty-two times. I would've played on the line, except my uncle was the coach."

"I was a tackle," I told him.

A queasy pause engulfed us as the wind whipped through the sleet. I scraped my foot back and forth, clearing out a small space in the snow. "Twins, huh?"

His lips spread into a wide grin. "Yessir, twin boys. Rudy, he was the first one. You never saw such a hairy baby. And big—that boy was almost nine pounds. Maybe he'll play some football, like me and you. Then after graduation, I can just see us running the farm together, spending our weekends hunting and fishing." He went on talking as he shifted his weight. "Now the other one, Jack, he's a lot smaller. Most babies have this wrinkled

28

kind of skin, but not that boy. No, Jack's smooth and fair, almost pale looking. And he has this twinkle in his eyes. I swear, they're a copy of his momma's baby blues. That boy's gonna be a real lady-killer when he grows up. Why, he'll probably have a couple of wives and a dozen kids." He smacked those old gloves together and his smile grew wider. "Listen to this: Jack came out holding onto the leg of the first one, like he was trying to crawl over him so he wouldn't be the second one out. Isn't that something? Whoever heard of such a thing? Twin boys," he said, and I could see his eyes traveling out through time to some bright distant pride those twin boys might bring him. But then, it was as if a cloud passed over that future sunshine, and he remembered the jam he was in under the neon. He didn't even have the money to get that family of his back to Willingboro. When he looked back at me, his eyes had a look that told me we had returned to our original topic of conversation.

I briefly thought about checking my pockets for change, but I didn't bother. What's he going to do with a quarter—call the gas station and ask them for a loan? So I did what most honest men would do in my situation: I stalled some more. "You know," I said, "it's funny how you remember things. I remember when I was a kid in Sunday School. You know, I haven't thought about this in years. I remember somebody telling me how Jewish people believed Jesus was a twin. Imagine that. I can't remember if it was a teacher or another kid that fed me that one." He didn't say anything, so I kept on. "You know, Elvis Presley was a twin. His twin was born dead. They say Elvis never got over that. He always wondered why he lived and his brother had died."

"No. I didn't know that. I never cared much for his music." His voice was softer, far away, resigned. He understood that I wasn't inclined to give him anything. Maybe he was starting to think of a different way to get that money.

Another silence from the night settled on the two of us. So what was I supposed to do? I could have asked about his wife, or why the hell they had come all the way down here from Willingboro. Naturally, I didn't think of that until much later. And then, without even thinking, I felt my right hand reaching into my back pocket and lifting out my wallet. Stupid fool, I thought to myself. I was bewildered and embarrassed. Suppose, while I'm looking into my wallet, he clubs me over the head and takes the whole thing with my driver's license, my ID, and everything else? And what was Sally going to say, with all our bills coming in at the end of the month, and next month's rent falling due soon, when she discovered that I had given away some of our hard-earned money to a stranger from somewhere near Willingboro? I tried to swallow, but my sad mouth was dry.

There were just two bills inside my wallet—a pair of Andrew Jacksons—both shiny and new. I shook my head and whispered, "Oh Lord." But I reached into my wallet and plucked out one of those twenties. Maybe it was the cold and the snow, or maybe it was his slippery wet shoes, or maybe it was all he carried, as if his story might possibly be true. After all, who would make up a story like that? Sometimes, I sighed to myself, life is simply trusting without knowing.

As I handed him the twenty dollars, I looked at him hard and straight in the eye, but I didn't say anything except, "Good luck." I guess I wanted him to know that if this was a con, I suspected as much. Could he understand that if I revealed my suspicion, I somehow recaptured my dignity, if not my money? I don't know. The honest truth is, I believed the man; either that, or I had talked myself into believing him. But whichever it was, he had my twenty dollars.

He looked at the bill, tucked it into his trouser pocket, and then he raised his surprised eyes up to mine. He paused for a second before he spoke in that same quiet and dignified voice. "Thank you, sir. Thank you very much. You are truly one kind-hearted man. I hope you and your family have yourselves a wonderful holiday and a real good new year."

I just nodded and decided if he was a con man, he was a damn good one. But then I felt a little lighter inside, felt pretty good, because I knew it was my twenty bucks that would get his family home, and with luck, it might even stretch part of a tiny Christmas dinner across their table. Of course, it wouldn't go too far for his wife and those twin boys; but there wasn't anything I could do about that.

As I twisted around and opened my car door, he walked away. I bent over to slip inside, but on an impulse I suddenly straightened up and called out to him, "You take good care of those twins." He stopped in his tracks and looked back at me. I could see his big white grin shining through the evening turned to night; and over the ping of sleet bouncing off my rooftop, I heard the unleashed joy erupting from his laughter.

NIGHT SHIFT LEGENDS

For Damon, the beginnings are identical: Across the top skip streaks of colors, staccato dabs of blues and reds and yellows. The lower celluloid is clear and the projector highlights a ragged tear on the screen. Abruptly, tear and screen are submerged under huge, grainy numbers, 5—4—3, each one circled by a minute hand spinning the hour back from later towards now. Then there is darkness. From speakers built into the ceiling hisses and crackles slide into a saxophone theme. He knows from the others in this series of films that it's Jamestown who's playing, and he smiles, acknowledging the return of his melodious old friend. In his head the sax line swells, then drifts away. The outside of a bathroom door replaces the dark screen he's imagined, and so, completely returned to where he is, Damon raises his hand and softly knocks.

Lisa looks away from the urinal. Someone once told her that in France men and women share the same public bathrooms. Would it be strange if she lived in Paris, her eyes ask the mirror. In Paris she would be his mistress, her eye shadow would remain in perfect crescents, and over baskets of bread in the pâtisserie she would nod to his wife, but say nothing. She would work days and never, never, have to rotate to nights. But this is not Paris and this mirror, with cracks splintery as spider legs creeping down one side, hangs on the bathroom wall of the male physician's lounge. It's not her first time with Damon, but it's their first time here, and she wishes he'd arrive. Anyone could walk in now. Anyone.

As if they didn't already know, as if the whole goddam hospital didn't already know.

Naturally, he's late. She's hurried through the past hour of work, checking her watch often, and slipped into the lounge three minutes early. That was twenty minutes ago. She knows his excuse will be as tenderly crafted as ballet: a conference with a patient's tearful family, a sick child who suddenly who needed his attention—as if he were the only doctor here. And he'll know which steps to avoid. Damon never comes to Lisa from his wife. She should never have let him talk her into this. It's not that she's prissy, but she's always been conscientious about her work.

"It's something I've always wanted to do," he'd said, gently massaging her neck as she clocked in at 11:00. Then he'd turned her around and resting his hands on her thin shoulders, his blue eyes teasing her, he'd curled his lips into a smile. "Can't you see how magnificent it would be? To screw our brains out inside this stinking hospital." A lock of brown hair tumbled onto his forehead. "And tonight's perfect. Nothing's happening."

"I love it when you sweet talk me that way."

"Oh baby," he said, kissing her neck.

"Oh baby yourself," she answered pushing him away.

But here she is. She's given up trying to understand why she loves him. With her, love is always an accident, a flaming collision. She tries to be honest with herself, and there are moments when she knows the only reason for believing this will turn out differently from her previous loves is her tremendous desire that it should. Still, she plans each day so she is certain to see him.

She brushes smooth her short black hair, straightens the bangs above her eyes, then turns sideways to the mirror. Her chin is too sharp in profile, her neck too long. She tells the glass, "If humiliation was gasoline you'd make one hell of a torch."

A knock is followed by a husky whisper calling through the door, "Lisa? Are you there? Lisa?"

Her heart swells as it does whenever she hears him say her name. She smiles at the mirror, brushes a few strands that were already in place, murmurs "Idiot," then louder she answers Damon as casually as she can, "Just a minute."

Damon lowers the side rail, thankful that the name on his clipboard matches the one taped to the head of the crib. He opens the oxygen tent and ducks his head inside, waving through the mist until he sees the sleeping child.

He raises the patched fringe of her gown, turns on his flashlight, and sees the beads of mist and feverish sweat glistening on her chest. Her breath blows raspy, an uneasy churning, and when he presses his stethoscope against her slippery hot skin, a gurgle of thick mucous rattles in his ears. He considers increasing her oxygen or changing antibiotics but decides neither would hasten her recovery, and satisfied, he smooths the child's gown, straightens the covers around her, then backs out of the tent and seals the zipper.

He checks his watch, and seeing it's 3:15 he sighs, but approaches the window anyhow. He gazes at the park across the street, looking for signs of Jamestown, though when he comes he's seldom more than twenty minutes late. Damon is now the chief resident, but since the earliest days of his internship he has paused while making his rounds to scan the concrete park. There, beneath a towering cluster of lights, Jamestown Edison blows his sax. He is an augury for Damon. When Jamestown misses a performance, no one hawks poisoned candy at the schools. Divine inspiration steers drunks safely down the interstate. The usually active Knife and Gun Club postpones all ritual sacrifices. Naturally, the average citizen would be pleased with this confluence, but for Damon it adds up to a wasted, boring night. "Looks like a quiet one," he murmurs, blowing a cloud upon the glass. "But on the other hand, you got to hammer Lisa in the lounge."

A voice calls from behind him, "Dr. T., how's that Martinez baby sound tonight?"

He turns and sees the plump silhouette of Zoretta framed in the doorway. "Her breathing's improved. The pneumonia's resolving." She nods her approval and turns to leave when Damon remembers. "How's Darnell's pressure?"

She stops, resting her back against the door, and kneads a cranky hip. She's been caring for the children here since before Damon was born and her joints ache from all those years of bending over infants, and lifting and rocking, feeding and changing them. She says, "Okay for now. Poor boy. What kind of chance you think he's got?"

"For a third transplant? About the same chance you've got of going to the moon."

"That's what I heard."

"Yeah, it's too bad. He's a nice kid."

She passes into the hallway, shaking her head. "Ain't it always that way?"

Darnell is sixteen and rejecting his second transplanted kidney. The

33

medicines aren't working, and unfortunately, the rules are pretty clear: no one who has rejected twice has ever been given a third. Damon remembers the night of Darnell's last surgery. A light airy feeling percolated through the ICU. Everyone liked Darnell. Bloated and miserable though he was from his nephritis and its treatment, Darnell would joke with the staff when he felt well and wouldn't whine too much when he didn't. He was constantly trying to sneak around the rules restricting his diet and activities, and he was never successful. When apprehended he pouted, insistently unrepentant, but he remained a favorite because his adolescent pride never quite concealed his shy embarrassment at being caught.

Damon was in a good mood when he entered Darnell's room before the operation. The examination was little more than a formality. He had inspected Darnell's body so many times he knew exactly what he would find: a pink flabby abdomen crossed by valleys of surgical scars, thick mottled thighs, arms swollen and pocked with bruises that were shaggy rings of purple and tarnished copper green. At first, Darnell seemed indifferent to the excitement surrounding him. He moved listlessly and kept his eyes closed through much of the examination. When Damon teased or asked him a question, the reply was a muffled grunt. Damon guessed he was anxious about the surgery, but afterwards, as Damon was stooped over the sink washing his hands, Darnell said, "I'm never going back to dialysis."

"Well, you know sometimes a new kidney can't take on a full load right away. It might need some help."

"No, that's not what I mean. I mean if this kidney ends up like the last one, no one's putting me back on that machine."

Damon saw the determination in his puffy eyes, and answered quietly, "Let's see what happens." But he knew then Darnell would keep his word. He had seen children make and keep these promises before. And so that same night, even as Darnell was receiving his kidney, Damon—never a great optimist—began shaping a final contingency plan. Now, if he can only arrange the logistics.

The hospital is a rising cylinder with a central atrium hollowed out of the core. The cap of the atrium is a dynamic, geodesic glass dome, a lens that on clear days funnels sunlight down to windows on the inner wards. They look down onto a polished tile lobby that's designed to have the warm feeling of an open courtyard, and there are large wooden planters holding the roots of several bamboo trees surrounded by myrtles and peace lilies. Lisa, skeptical any tree could possibly thrive there, once climbed onto a planter and touched one. She was startled when the smooth bark wasn't plastic, though she hasn't dismissed the possibility that an administrator substitutes fresh trees at night, when no one is looking. The remaining windows open onto outside vistas. They look down onto rows of torn tenement shades or face the flat concrete park across the street, a cheap renovation of a dead city block. One night Damon explained that there were scientific studies proving that patients with windows in their rooms required fewer painkillers than their windowless counterparts. At the time she never thought to ask if they found any difference between those who face inside and those who look out. She rubs her fingertips through her bangs. It's a question that would intrude upon her only when she's working nights. She hates it. Working nights is like landing in a foreign country she never wanted to visit: it's exotic, annoying, and incredibly tiring.

She's pushing a med cart down the hall, her fingers unconsciously tapping the handle in time with the cart's steady jingle, when one foot trips over the other. She plunges onto the handle and the jingle becomes a clanging just before the swerving cart smashes into a doorway. Pain sears along her ribcage. She bites her lower lip, stifling a cry. Her eyes stare at the base of the short front leg where a wheel twirls aimlessly.

She tries to believe it's not a punishment; the world doesn't work that way. She spins the cart around, and cautioned by pain, she slowly returns to the nursing station. When she rounds the corner she finds Roxanne, one of the usual night nurses, sitting at the desk flipping through the pages of Playgirl. "Don't you people think of anything but sex?"

"Not on purpose," Roxanne answers. She has meticulously layered auburn hair, sly brown eyes with long lashes, and a quick warm smile. She claims she's a refugee from the hills, though which hills nobody knows. Lisa understands why Roxanne would never fit in any dirt road town. She keeps no secrets. Even Lisa, who's never cared much for gossip and barely knows her, has heard how some of the night staff stumbled onto Roxanne screwing Jimmy D. in an isolation room, and just a few days ago she heard Damon and some friends speculating on who might have assisted Roxanne in losing the anklet found that morning beneath an OR table.

Roxanne asks, "What do you read? The newspaper?"

Zoretta pokes her head around the corner. "Darnell's pressure's up to 160 over 94. Roxanne, you still have his Apresoline?"

"Damn, I left it in the cart. I'll get it now." She pushes herself up from the desk and tosses the magazine to Lisa. The man on the cover has a nice smile. "Feast your eyes on him."

Lisa mumbles a tired, "Thanks," and fills a mug with coffee. She sinks into the chair, holding the cup so the steam rises and warms her face. After a few breaths she opens her eyes, but Zoretta and Roxanne are gone. She sets down the cup and opens the magazine. A naked man is standing in a brown autumn forest, one foot poised upon the trunk of a thick, fallen oak. So strong, jaunty and brash, he looks as if he just felled the huge tree by himself. Lisa notices the stray lock of hair on his forehead is curled just like Damon's.

"Not bad, is he?" Roxanne laughs as she returns.

"No, not bad at all. How's Darnell?"

"Darnell? He's the same. I just hope Damon gets his plan together in time."

Lisa looks back at the magazine, quickly turns a few pages.

"Don't you like the idea? I sure hope it's one night when I'm working."

"Oh, that would be fun."

For the last month Damon has been cruising the cafeteria, pulling aside potential sponsors for his "Magical Evening of Delight." It's an all-expenses-paid cruise to fantasyland for Darnell, a visit from the most expensive call girl he can find. Lisa's watched him leave their cafeteria table to go buttonhole likely donors. He reminds her of an insurance salesman. "Think of it as a package deal," he says in an ingratiating tone, "a two-fer, a combination going away present and apology things have worked out the way they have."

She tells Roxanne, "I hear they've raised $400."

Roxanne rests her hands on her hips and contemplates, "Imagine that. Imagine what they can buy for $400. Imagine what you and I could buy for $400."

Lisa pauses, then says earnestly, "I can't see paying a guy for it. Would you? Would you really do that?"

"Who knows? If the circumstances were right, maybe I would. Don't you like to try different things? Sometimes, I just feel like busting right out of my skin."

Busting right out of my skin. Few things would scare Lisa more than this. Her dreams are of cozy containment, of being safely wrapped up. "I think I'd be too self-conscious to enjoy it."

"Well, that's why they have chocolate and vanilla in the ice cream store. To each his own. Different strokes for different folks, and all that."

No longer listening, Lisa lifts her cup and rocks it gently. She peeks over the rim and watches the swirling coffee lick the sides of the mug, then quickly she drains it. She dabs her lips with a tissue then looks up to find Roxanne watching her and she feels embarrassed, though she's not sure why. As she rises she says, "Well, I guess it's time to give out some drugs."

"Yes, I suppose we've both got a lot left to do."

Damon is padding down a hallway where the sun yellow walls are covered with painted clowns and tangles of balloons. The corridor is empty except for a broken railed crib nosing from a storage closet doorway and an old EKG machine some intern abandoned in the middle of the hall. His mind starts to wander and then his rubber sole squeaking against linoleum becomes a trigger: he's back in the movies. These films are classic sagas. They roll across the screen the way stars slowly cross the black night sky. Tonight's feature is, *NIGHT SHIFT LEGENDS*. This is Damon making rounds. What an exciting, reassuring series of adventures! By the time the house lights go up at the end, you're sure to feel dizzy and dazzled and envious of the hero. Practically raising them from the dead, a handsome young doctor saves the lives of incredibly sick children in a busy city hospital. Jamestown Edison's score is magnificent. Damon Topolopolous, Nastassia Kinski. Five stars. Here's the shot: He's leaving the bed after screwing Lisa. She's pouting reluctance while he, proud fist upon his chest, reminds her of his oath to the sick. Then there's a little flash of tit to really grab the viewer's interest. His mind's eye still sees Lisa's breasts when he realizes she is actually pushing her med cart down the hall towards him. He's impressed with the power of suggestion. "I was just thinking of you."

"I bet."

"I was. I think about you all the time. I was on my way to check Darnell. Want to come along?"

She looks at the cart and thinks of all the work she has to do. She says, "Sure. Why not?"

They stop abruptly as Damon opens the door. Darnell's bed is rocking, springs groaning with strain. An undulating orange halo from a flashlight hovers above his blankets. Damon grins, begins to pull the door shut, but Lisa stops him. "It could be a seizure," she insists, pushes past him, and tiptoes briskly across the floor. At the bed she leans over, placing her lips a few inches above where Darnell's ears should be. "Darnell," she whispers loudly.

The blanket jumps up, Lisa hops back, and a huffing, pale face appears. Its eyes are glossy moons. "What?" he gasps.

"Are you okay?"

"Of course I'm okay. Leave me alone." He yanks the covers over his head.

She stands beside the bed, hands clasped behind her back. "I thought you might...a seizure sometimes...I'm really sorry I disturbed you." As she expects, there is no answer, and she retreats to the hall.

Damon pulls the door shut behind her. "Satisfied?"

Lisa's watery eyes ache. Everyone knows she's a good nurse. Each line on her face is paved with good intentions. "What if he'd been having a seizure? From across the room it could look the same."

"Four years out of nursing school and you can't tell a seizure from masturbation? Maybe you should return for some brushing up."

"I'm only trying to do what's right." Then she looks away, lets her eyes rest on a spool of paper winding off the EKG machine onto the floor. "You know that. You know I'm only trying to do what's right. Why do you treat me this way?"

"Which way were you thinking of?"

"It's about this fabulous prank of yours, isn't it? This stupid, jerky, adolescent prank. 'Let's see if we can sneak a hooker inside without getting caught.' If you really cared about Darnell, you'd think about what your hooker could do to his blood pressure." She shakes a fist at the ceiling. "This whole thing is sick."

"I'm surprised you take such a dim view of sex on the premises."

"You're so proud of yourself, aren't you?"

He lets out a long breath. "Look, you're always saying I'm only thinking about myself, but what if we give him a choice? What if we say, 'Darnell, you can die a virgin or you can take this last chance to discover the ultimate earthly bliss.' Which do you think he'll choose?"

"He's sixteen. He's under the influence of very powerful hormones."

"I can't change that."

"It could kill him."

"Let him decide."

"But you're his doctor. You're not supposed to let your patients kill

38

themselves."

"It's not as if I can save him."

"But what about another transplant? What about dialysis?"

"Lisa, another kidney is a billion-to-one shot. And he's not going back on dialysis. I can promise you that."

"He could change his mind."

"No," he says with quiet assurance. "He's not going to change his mind."

"It's not right, Damon, it's just not right. None of it. None of this is right." She suddenly feels tears approaching that she won't let him see. She pirouettes as gracefully as she can and, chin high, sweeps down the hall towards the nursing station.

Damon watches her with cold eyes. "Fuck you," he mutters, not sure who's supposed to hear him.

Roxanne snaps her wrist, shaking two packets of sugar which she then rips open. Her eyes oscillate between Lisa's twitching eyes and the sweet white falls she pours into her coffee. Finally, she says, "You remember that movie, *Close Encounters of the Third Kind*? That magazine we were reading had a sort of follow up on it, interviewing people that claim to have had personal experiences with aliens."

Except for the two nurses the cafeteria is deserted. A ring of soft lights shines down on the empty lunch counter. Lisa turns her bleary gaze from the sharp pools of glistening chrome. "Oh?"

"One guy, some banker from Montana, claims he was kidnapped by aliens and taken to their spaceship for a physical. The police found him wandering naked in the desert near Las Vegas."

Lisa squints at her, hoping to see if she is serious or not. "Well," she begins cautiously, "you don't have to be an Einstein to figure that one out."

"Right," Roxanne laughs, "but then some yoyo journalist turns up this scientist from NASA who analyzed this jelly they found on the banker. He says he discovered something in that jelly—something, what did he call it?— something like 'polyglycopolylate'—anyway, it's ten times more powerful than any lubricant known to man. And now the government's hushing him up so he can't tell anybody about it. Now, why would they muzzle that scientist if he wasn't telling the truth?"

Lisa's so tired, the rubber band she's spun around herself and Damon has popped and stung her, and now Roxanne is babbling this incredible nonsense. She buries her face in her hands. "I don't know."

Roxanne pauses, stirs her coffee and says nothing. She takes a sip. Her full lips curl at the taste, still acrid despite the sugar. "Damn," she sighs. "You want to talk about it?"

"The UFO?"

"Or Damon."

"I wouldn't know what to say. About either one."

While waiting to hear if Lisa means this or not, Roxanne considers, then selects two packets of Sweet'n'Low. As she stirs them into the coffee, she says thoughtfully, "Going against my better sense, let me give you a little friendly advice. You can take this any way you want—you can forget it if you want— anyway, whenever I find myself falling for a guy who's gonna be trouble, I imagine him doing the most repulsive, disgusting things I can think of. And then I imagine it over and over until I convince myself it's true, that he really has done it. And after that, the spell is broken. I'm a free woman again."

Lisa supposes she means well, but is irritated at the intrusion. "I'm not like you," she says. "I mean, I wish it would all be so easy for me."

"Don't make things more difficult than they have to be. Don't worry about things that don't need worrying over."

"I'm just not the way you are."

Roxanne's cup slips for a second, but she steadies it before any coffee spills. Her expression is one of pity and bewilderment, a milder version of the smile she has for infants too young to understand pain. She says, "Just try it. Just use your imagination."

"It doesn't work that way. My imagination."

Roxanne pauses then asks, "Tell me, Lisa, what would you do if a spaceship landed and the king of the UFOs asked you to fly away with him and be his mistress? Would you do it? Would you fly away to be the mistress of the king of the sky?"

Lisa finally raises her eyes. She looks at Roxanne, but sees no light dancing in those brown eyes and says, "I doubt it. Not that I have any plans, but I doubt it. Would you?"

"In...a...minute," puffs Roxanne, each word an imaginary wreath rising to the ceiling. "In...a...minute."

The first night Damon heard Jamestown, one of his first nights on call, his chest tightened with panic and disappointment. Room by room he searched the corridors for the source of the eerie music, but once inside the rooms became interchangeable: a child wheezing under an oxygen tent, a silent television bolted upon the wall, and in the air that music, the singularly pure and piercing call of a saxophone. Exhausted—this was his third straight night without sleep—he thought about the ominous strain of a movie soundtrack, the warning a hero is not supposed to hear. At last, he happened to glance out a window and found his answer in the park under a hot yellow cone of streetlight. Coiled and twisted around his saxophone, a huge, muscular Black man rocked back, paused, and glistening tense, shot life itself flying down the tube of his horn. Of all the goddam times to hallucinate, he thought. Four weeks into his internship and he'd already lost it. Washed out at twenty-five. He took a deep breath, his drained eyes staring at the glass. A weaker man might have cried. He barely moved when Zoretta tapped him on the shoulder. "He's something, that boy. Right on time again."

Damon let his breath out slowly. "No kidding. Who is he?"

"Jamestown Edison, serenading the whores across the street."

"The whores?"

"They don't tell you rookies nothing 'portant about this place." She chuckled in a hoarse, low voice and pressed a fat finger against the window. "That house with the purple light on, that's the one. Some say Jamestown got a girl there. He's out here most every night to play, trying to win her heart back."

And Damon, a bit less cynical at that time, found he admired the persistence and grace of Jamestown's mission. For several minutes he remained with Zoretta at the window, flowing with the music until his beeper summoned him from his reverie.

A few hours after that first performance, Damon was sitting in the empty emergency room when a mother rushed in with a limp, blue toddler. With the cool demeanor of a carnival magician he extracted the sticky wad of sausage blocking her windpipe. Within seconds her face was pink again. Her mother cried tears of relief and gratitude. A stunned class of nursing students stared in amazement, then cooed and cheered until he blushed. Throughout the day his fellow interns offered their grudging congratulations. It was Damon's first great act of heroism, and ever since that night, whenever he's in the hospital at 3 a.m., he will stop by the window and wait, hoping to hear the sonorous, lilting agony that Jamestown Edison blows.

When they arrive there is no heartbeat, no respiration. Roxanne watches Damon lift up the eyelids and they both see the right pupil is three times larger than the left. They know instantly: a blood vessel burst in the brain, and there was hemorrhaging, a swelling that forced the medulla through the opening in the base of his skull. The respiratory center has been destroyed. There is nothing that can save him.

Without hesitation Damon begins to run the code. An intern helps him pull and tug the flaccid body until it's tilted enough for Lisa to slide a flat board underneath. The intern begins chest compressions, pounds steadily, pausing only when Damon injects Darnell's heart with one of the long needled cardiac syringes. As he pushes down the plunger Damon calmly announces to Zoretta taking notes the ritual sequence of medications: epinephrine, bicarbonate, glucose; epinephrine, bicarbonate, glucose. After every fifth compression, Roxanne squeezes a bulbous plastic bag sending a pulse of oxygen into a tube lowered through his mouth into his lungs.

Quick and precise they act smoothly. There is no urgency here, no suspense. Each of them knows this attempt to revive Darnell is both correct and sure to fail. Whatever excitement ripples through the room is but a tremor of escape, a tickling at the fringe of mortality, a wave that washes across the living whenever death is a nearby visitor.

After ten minutes Damon steps away and gently pulls the intern's sweat-soaked arm. "Enough," he says. "That's enough."

In the lounge they lie cuddled in a lover's spoon. Damon's facing the wall, his eyes resting on the familiar spot where someone's fingernail has picked a hole. He notices for the first time a faded edge of wallpaper chipped clean of olive paint and wonders when the paper was covered.

"Look," she says, "We knew he was going to die. It was just a question of when. You saw his eyes. What could you do?"

He understands her point, though it doesn't change the fact that Darnell now lies in the morgue. But what's really troubling him is that he wants to ask her if Jimmy D., if anyone in the history of the hospital, has ever bagged two nurses in one night, only he can't find the right way to phrase the question. He says, "Lisa was right."

"About what?"

"My plan for Darnell. It would've killed him. We caught him masturbating twenty minutes before the code. I'm sure that's what did it."

For a moment she silently considers what he's said. "Well, didn't your mother ever warn you about the evils of masturbation? Mine sure did."

"Oh did she?"

"She sure did. That's when I figured out what my friends were for." Roxanne rolls over and her fingers begin to prowl along his thigh. "Damon, let's be friends."

He lowers his mouth to hers and quickly her fingers are tugging on the drawstring of his scrub pants. Her greedy hands snake inside, and fingers stroke him fast, implore him urgently. "Now," she tells him. "Now." Her wetness blossoms against his thigh. Once inside, he feels her quickly climax. He clutches her tightly, flows with the waves of his own diminishing spasms, then slides free of her, resting between her breasts, listening to their synchronous breathing sweetly gliding slowly down. He hears her heart, imagines the whirr of a camera rolling and, as if on cue, a soaring wail of saxophone slices through the blanket of the night.

For you, he silently tells Darnell, for you. It's not the first time he's hoped a message might reach the other side. If you can hear me, Darnell, this night's episode is for you.

It's cold. At the window Lisa shivers and watches the lavender curtain of horizon rise to unveil a luminous orange dawn. The orange of a fire, she thinks, and whispers, "It should burn both of them." She shivers once more. She shuts her eyes and tells herself it must happen again as it has happened before. Pain is always the first step towards indifference. One day that fire won't burn, one day that wind won't blow. One day he won't matter. One day Damon Topolopolous won't matter at all.

She opens her eyes to scan the dawning light, but she's distracted by Jamestown in the distance leaving the park. What a swagger! With his sax case tucked under one arm, he struts into the morning, dancing half-turns and tipping his hat, bending his knee now and then in a sharp dipsy-do. What can he know, she wonders. What can he know? Her smile is like a sliver of the moon. She waits until he's disappeared, then raising her hands she applauds.

CATCH A WAVE

I had borrowed that baby blue surfboard, so when I picked her up I was a live wire ready to spark. It was a perfect day: the sky was clear and a soft breeze was blowing from the northeast. When there was no wind at all, the swells were fat and lazy, but this breeze was strong enough to get the surf up, to make those swells sharp and crisp. I could picture those surfers riding the waves, and I wanted to ride one too. That day, more than anything else in the world, I wanted to ride the crest of a crashing wave.

Carol was wearing cut offs and a blue work shirt over her bathing suit. She brought along the suntan lotion, some fruit and sandwiches, and a People magazine. I brought that surfboard and a cooler full of PBR. "Natalie thinks she's pregnant," Carol told me. Natalie was a sharp looking brunette who worked with Carol at the mall. They sold gold chains and necklaces in the jewelry department at Sears. "She doesn't know what to do."

"Shoot. Only one thing to do. What's she going to do with a baby?"

"Easy for you to say," she answered as she plucked a grape out of the bag and slipped it between my lips. "Like you could ever know what she's feeling. And you know her folks are Catholic. Can you imagine what her Daddy'd do? I hate to think about it."

"I'm glad it's not my problem."

"Yeah, me too." She chuckled. "I can just picture you and Natalie stuck together for life."

We went to the north end of the beach, the same place we always went, which was just off 88th Street right before you get to the fence at Fort Story. I had taken her there on our very first date the summer before, and after a summer of weekends on that stretch of sand, we had come to consider it our own special beach, even though we did have to share it with whoever showed up on any particular day.

She read her magazine while I sat next to her, waxing the board and sucking on a beer. The beach was crowded, like it should be on a hot Saturday in August. So many people were swimming and wading in the ocean that I couldn't even think of trying to surf. It was as if God's little finger had lifted up the western tip of Virginia and all the people had tumbled down until they landed at the beach. Flabby old men with grey haired chests slumped down in their beach chairs trying to ignore their wives who were squawking back and forth like gulls. Sailors, I knew they had to be sailors because no one else would wear their hair that short, were stacking up a pyramid of empty beer cans and trying to pick up girls. And everywhere sandy little kids were screaming, whooping and hollering at each other, while toddlers ran around in their droopy diapers. I fastened my eyes on a sweet thing sauntering through the surf in the flimsiest excuse for a bikini that you could ever hope to see, and took another long, hard swallow.

Carol asked me to rub some lotion on her back, but when I tried to slip my hand too low she got all wiggly and said, "Not here. Not in front of all these people."

I took my hand away and cracked open another beer. Towards late afternoon, the crowd began to leave. One by one, I saw the surfers appear in the water, perched beyond the breakers on their boards. They paddled in wide circles, talking to each other, eyeing the waves. Suddenly splashing huge butterfly strokes, one shot off in a frenzy through the ocean. I watched him slide along the crest of the swell as it rose and broke beneath him. He shimmied along the board, keeping a graceful balance, and he rode that wave until it died near the shore. When he hopped off the surfboard, he shook the water out of his hair, and then he swam out to join the others. Carol had watched him too. "You'll never see a fat surfer," she told me; and she was right. I didn't mind her watching the surfers. After all, what's fair is fair. At last, I decided my own personal inexperience would not pose a danger to humanity, and I picked up the freshly waxed board.

The ocean water was cool and green with frothy whitecaps. I nosed the board into the waves and paddled out beyond the breakers. For a time I straddled the board and watched the folks on the shore. The sea was so quiet compared to the crowded beach that I felt like I was peeking at those people through a window with its shutters drawn. I was unseen and invisible.

Then three billowing swells rolled in towards me. I edged that board into the first wave and felt it catch, felt the surge lift me into its crest and carry me with it. When I tried to jump from my knees to my feet I pushed down too hard on one side of the board. It veered sharply, spilling me over, and treating me to a mouthful of ocean on the way down. When I came back up to the surface, I waved to Carol and paddled out to go another round.

Carol had put down her magazine to watch me. She was wearing a snug yellow two-piece suit, and in my eyes she was the most bewitching girl on the beach. With my large sunglasses perched on her nose, she may have been the silliest looking one as well. I knew she was worried the board would smack me on the head when I fell. "And then I'll have to find somebody to drag you out. I'm not going in there after you and get myself swallowed up by the ocean. The way you surf," she laughed nervously, "You'll end up on a stretcher at Bayside before you catch a wave."

She had a point, for I did have some crazy acrobatic falls: somersaults, belly flops, twists off the side. I might have lowered the Atlantic a few inches that day, with all the water I took in my mouth and up my nose. And she laughed every time I fell, but if she thought I stayed under the water too long, she would arch her back and scan the ocean, her hand in a crooked salute to shield the glasses from the glare. Then I would rise up spitting ocean, and she would lower her arm and laugh at me.

I rode exactly one wave that day. I wasn't on my feet for long, but I knew that feeling of being in the crest, that feeling of being alive without thinking. I just kept my balance as I rode that wondrous wave, and for all of ten seconds, I was in true harmony with the great green ocean. And then, of course, I fell.

After I had been falling for an hour, I needed to ease the briny taste. I swam ashore to Carol and we sipped our beers in silence. It was that time of day I wish would last forever. The lower sun behind us unveiled the golden highlights of the cooling sand. The high skyed wispy clouds carried in their wakes the pinks and violets of the late afternoon. A cool breeze scuttled across my shoulders, sending gooseflesh running down my spine. I pulled my darling tight to me and hugged her. I felt empty and full of happiness at the same time. She hugged me back and said, "I'm hungry."

We decided to eat at my favorite seafood place at the south end of the beach. When we arrived, the hostess showed us to a table on the outside deck that gave us a view of Rudee Inlet where it empties into the ocean. The inlet has a narrow channel protected by two uneven sloping walls of slate blue boulders that hold back the sand from washing in and closing it. Since there isn't a beach to speak of, it isn't any good for swimming, but lots of folks who like to fish will spend a day there. By supper time, the only people left fishing were a half a dozen Black men squatting on the other side of the channel. One of them was gesturing with his big hands and talking while the rest watched the water and their fishing lines. We couldn't hear them over the smoky droning engines of the fishing trawlers trudging home. Those long thin boats, their patched nets draped over the side, glided so slowly through the channel we could read the names carefully penned across the sides of their bows. Each trawler had a name like "Christine Roberta" or "Nancy Lee."

"Do you think they name their boats after their wives?" Carol asked me as she dipped into her she-crab soup.

"Probably. How about a taste of that soup? Would you like to have a boat named after you?"

She handed me a soup spoon full and said, "If it was your boat I would. I wouldn't want anyone else to name a boat after me. Well, maybe a big yacht. That would be ok." I had finished my fried seafood platter and hushpuppies when she pointed at a swirling of gulls darting behind a boat. "Look at those seagulls. All they do is eat and fly-."

"That can't be all they do, or else there wouldn't be any more seagulls."

"You," she laughed. "Those are nasty birds. I read all about them in the Sunday magazine. They're scavengers. They would rather steal from another bird than catch their own food. Look." She pointed to a bird with a fish hanging from its beak that was being chased by a bigger gull. "He won't catch him. That little one's too smart for him," she said with satisfaction.

She was interrupted by a peal of laughter that rolled across the inlet. The guy that had been talking must have finished his story because the others were grinning and laughing and taking turns slapping the big man's palm. I don't know how many fish they caught that day, but from where I sat, it didn't seem to matter too much. They just seemed to be relaxing and having a good time. I looked over at Carol. She had been so busy watching those fellows while she ate her dessert that she didn't realize she had left a thread of hot fudge dangling from her lower lip. I have kept a picture in my mind of her little girl embarrassment, her rosy cheeks and giggling eyes as we both laughed about that trail of hot fudge sundae. I was still laughing when I turned back to the men who were fishing, and somehow I knew they were just as happy as we were. And I was glad they were, too. I remember wishing at that very moment that everyone alive in the whole world could be as happy as those men and Carol and me.

When we finished supper, we cruised the avenue. The crowd that had jammed the beach during the day transformed the streets at night into a zoo.

Folks were everywhere. It took us a half hour to drive the twenty blocks from one end of the strip to the other. In the lane next to us a van was hot dogging between the red lights. Their music was so loud we could tell it was The Rondells singing on their radio. That van slowed down when it passed two cops prowling the beat. All the restaurants along the strip were full. Even the all-night pancake house, the one with the window so big you could look inside and watch the people eat, had a line snaking out the door and around the corner. Parents herded their kids through the ticky-tacky shops that sold the tourists paperweights, postcards, t-shirts and taffy. Carol pointed to a plump girl in a skimpy halter top. "Look at that top she's wearing," she said, trying to suppress a laugh. "When you eat like a hog, you can't dress like a fox."

"She's just fishing," I told her. "Just like everyone else out here. She's just fishing for a good time."

A little later we passed a swabby so drunk he had to wrap his arms around a lamp post to keep his balance. He yelled to Carol, "Hey girly!" and then belched so hard he almost fell over. "What's your name, you sweet thing?" She looked over at me, the color rising in her cheeks, and I just shook my head and we both laughed.

Down the road a neon sign was blinking "BINGO" into the night. I persuaded Carol that this was just the thing we were looking for and we parked the car. The bingo parlor was in a church. It was a sparsely decorated, rectangular room, and about fifty people were spread out among the long tables and folding chairs. We took our seats and a fat lady wearing an apron full of change and a pink sun visor that had "Bingo in the name of the Lord" printed on it sold me four cards for a dollar. Then the game began. An old man in a stiff white shirt drew the numbered balls from a rotating barrel. He would study the ball for a second to let the suspense build, and then he would holler the number in his cracked voice into the microphone. After so many numbers were called, somebody yelled, "Bingo. I got a bingo," and the lady with the apron waddled over to the winner and called off the winning numbers to make sure nobody had cheated. Then the old man said, "Another winner. Ladies and gents, we have another winner. Please clear your cards and we'll start a new game." Then he gave that barrel an extra sharp spin.

Two games running, I was one number away from a bingo when the same joker started screaming, "I won, I won." He was screaming so loud you would have thought he had won something important rather than a stupid bingo game. I was pissed off at having come so close but not winning. When I stuck my hand out to give the lady another dollar, Carol grabbed my arm and looked at me.

"Are you bored, honey?" I asked her. "Look, two games in a row, I almost won. I can't stop now. Come on, darling, let's play a little longer. I'm bound to win soon."

She didn't reply. She looked at me with eyes that said you're gonna do what you're gonna do, and it doesn't matter what I think anyway, so go ahead and do it. I said, "Thanks, honey. You just watch. One of us is going to win the next game."

And I started that next game like wildfire. I had four of the first six numbers. I was counting my winnings. It wouldn't be much, but maybe I could get us a hotel room at the beach. That was something I had always wanted: an oceanfront hotel room. We could have a glorious supper, then make love in that big hotel bed. In the morning we could have a room service breakfast and then go swimming in their private hotel pool.

Carol ignored her cards and was instead watching the couple sitting two tables in front of us. They looked like any another couple to me. I hadn't heard them say two words to each other since we arrived. "Aren't you going to watch your cards? You might have a winner."

"I'm not much of a bingo player," she said, still looking at that couple and ignoring me.

I tried to sound patient. "Well honey, all you've got to do is listen to the man call out the numbers and see if they're on your card. A four-year-old could do it. That's not too hard, is it?"

"Jack, I'm not a four year old. Maybe that's why I don't find it too exciting."

"Well, if you don't want to-" but then I stopped because the old man had called out a number that I knew was on one of my cards. I put the marker on it and I looked at her cards. She also had the number. "Look, you've got it too. Right there." I pointed to the spot on her plastic gamecard. She said nothing and pushed her cards over to my side of the table. I was so distracted by this that I missed five or six numbers and ended up losing the game to another screamer. I knew it was time to leave. I couldn't listen to any more screamers.

The night had grown hot and sticky when we emerged from the bingo parlor, and the thick crowd had become sullen and hungry. They were looking for something to break. Underneath a wave of neon lights, a pack of teenage boys passed around a bottle in a paper sack. When the bottle reached the smallest of the group and the runt tilted back his head to take a swig, a bigger

49

fellow laughed and snatched the bottle away from him. He took a long draw on it himself, and after wiping his wet grin on his sleeve, he gave the empty bottle back to his short friend. The rest of the group burst into mean laughter.

"Well, what does her highness want to do now? You want to go dancing at Peabody's? You want to do that? I know you can't be hungry again." But she wouldn't say anything and we stalked down Atlantic Avenue in a stormy silence. We squeezed through the crowd lined up outside the miniature golf course and I was so hot I almost tripped over a kid that was gawking at a storefront window. When we passed the amusement park, I crossed the street and jumped off the boardwalk onto the cool dark sand. She stayed up there for a minute, like she couldn't make up her mind, and then she slipped through the rail, slowly easing her way down to the beach. I called to her, "Come on, you won't break."

"I know I won't break," she answered back. It was the first thing she had said to me in twenty minutes. "I just don't want to get all sandy."

"You ain't going to dirty nothing that ain't been dirty before." But I was immediately sorry I said that, so I went back to her. I took her hand in mine and squeezed it. She paused, then squeezed back, and as we walked down the beach together, my anger was carried off by the sea breeze. The noise of the street faded into the sound of waves breaking on the shore.

She leaned into me and whispered, "Listen to the waves. I sat on the beach all day long and I didn't hear those waves once. Isn't that strange?"

"There's so much going on during the day. You've got those kids and their radios and the people talking. It's there, but it's like Muzak. You just don't think about it. I'll bet if you had closed your eyes and listened hard for a minute or two, you would have heard those waves."

"Maybe."

She let go of my hand, slipped her arm through mine, and leaned against my shoulder. We walked on the cool sand, past where the boardwalk gives way to the dunes, past the first of the rich people's houses, past the Navy Beach Club, and on into the night. As the bright glow of the city lights faded, the pale beach gained shape in the moonlight. The black shimmering ocean released a stronger salty breeze that sent her long hair blowing like silk against my face. I could have walked all night on that sand with her.

After we had walked awhile, we nestled in the dunes away from the breeze. I pulled her to me and raised her mouth to mine. I tasted the salt on her lips and I wanted to love her like I had never loved her before. We kissed and kissed again. I placed my hand outside her shirt, just testing, but she put her hand on top of mine and kissed me. "Not here, baby. Not now." I pulled my hand away and kissed her. What else did we have besides each other? What else did we need? If she didn't like bingo or surfing, we could find something else. That's what this life is all about. When one piece doesn't fit, you try another. After a few minutes we stood up and climbed the tallest dune. It wasn't very high, but from the top we could see far out on the ocean. There were buoys blinking in the distance, marking out a channel. The blinking seemed to be a coded message that I couldn't understand. I kept staring at those blinking lights until Carol tugged gently on my arm. We walked back towards the boardwalk. It would be awhile before we reached the crowd. She held my hand and we listened to the waves.

FORGET IT, JAKE

"No ma'am, we only rent out the movies. We don't service the machines...No, I've never had that problem with mine... Maybe you should look in the yellow pages...No problem...You too. Bye now." Abner looked at the clock as he hung up the phone. 11:30 and Dan was late for the third time this week. A less even-tempered man might show some annoyance, but Abner just shrugged his shoulders. If he asked, Dan would say he was meeting with his "investors."

Anyway, the store was empty. Few customers arrived before lunch. Abner stared through the "V" in the "Video Fields" plate glass window to watch the post office across the street. Sometimes a person's stride or clothing would so arouse his curiosity he would create a scenario: a young woman mails a letter to her favorite uncle in Alaska; the businessman in sunglasses conceals the parcel of satin sheets he wasn't expecting from his lover. "Sweet Jesus," Abner muttered at a scruffy, furtive little man: a letter bomb.

He was startled when the bell jingled. A frazzled woman, several months pregnant, trundled into the store with two children. They guided her along the narrow aisles between the racks jammed with the brightly colored cassette boxes. Abner chuckled silently at the thought of two tug boats maneuvering a battleship through a harbor.

"Smurfs. We want the Smurfs."

"But you watched the Smurfs last weekend."

"Smurfs, Smurfs. We want the Smurfs." Both children took up the chant.

The mother curled over her belly to study the bottom of the rack, but the Smurf movie was missing. "We can't watch the Smurfs today. Someone else has taken it. Wouldn't you like to see *Snow White*?"

"Smurfs, Smurfs. We want the Smurfs. Smurfs, Smurfs. We want the Smurfs." The cry grew louder as the mother pressed her palms against her strained lower back. Dan whisked through the door, coat open and flapping, his crown of blond hair bouncing with each large step. He glanced at the children and then tossed a knowing look to Abner. "Smurfs, Smurfs. We want the Smurfs." Without taking off his coat, Dan hopped behind the counter, reached under the register next to Abner and pulled out a cassette.

He waved it at the mother. "Mrs. Jackson."

Her face brightened with relief. "Oh, Dan. You're a lifesaver. I don't know what I would've done. Once they've made up their minds...." She spread her arms above the children and gave him a wry smile.

"No problem. I forgot to slip it back on the shelf when it came in yesterday. No wonder you couldn't find it."

"Well, thanks anyway." She checked out the cassette and shooed her children out of the store.

As soon as the door shut Dan said, "So Abner, how were the Smurfs last night?"

Abner's moon face entered its red harvest phase. "I was going to give it to her. I was reaching for it myself when you jumped over here."

Dan shook his head and grinned, "Right."

"Really. I was. I just wanted to see what would happen."

Dan retreated to the small office in the rear of the store and poured himself a coffee. Abner turned away from the tall lean figure and let his eyes rest on the racks, then rise to the pale orange walls that reflected the harsh brilliance of the overhead lights. Dan called out to him, "Abner Abnerovitch, are you ready for today's lesson?"

"I don't know. The lunch crowd will be here soon."

"A short one?"

Abner paused. "Ok."

Dan was fascinated with Russia. He seemed to have studied everything—books, movies, newspapers—that had even the vaguest connection with the country, and he would reveal small bits of his knowledge to Abner in each of these brief daily lessons. His driving ambition was to go to the Soviet Union and make a movie there. Abner was satisfied working in Mr. Field's video store; he loved to watch movies, all kinds of movies. But for Dan this was a temporary job. He was a different sort of dreamer. He had flown to Washington and spoken with a member of the Soviet Consul. He had applied for and received a visa. He had even saved enough money to buy some first rate video equipment; but after his purchases, he had no money left. He had neither cast nor crew. As far as Abner knew, he didn't even have a script.

"There's a plant not far from Moscow," Dan began. "A printing plant, where they put out these portraits of Lenin, Marx, you know, all the early heroes. Pictures you'd hang up in a classroom or a post office. Stuff like that." He took a big gulp of his coffee. "Well, there are five different portraits of each man. For instance, on the ones they send to the Mongol republics, Lenin has the slightest slant to his eyes, but the Cossacks see a man with straighter eyes and a stronger jaw. Just slight ethnic differences, but significant in their own way. Very typical of the Soviets, don't you think? That's the kind of thing I want to show."

"But that's exactly the kind of thing they won't let you film."

"Not if I show The Party in a positive light."

"How could you do that? It's such obvious duplicity."

"Not at all. Look at it as a unifying device. Think of all the different portraits we have of George Washington. All men have many faces. Who's to say which one is true? These men are the gods of the republic, and naturally, they reflect the features of their culture just like all other gods do. You'll never see a Buddha who looks western."

"You know what I'll never see? I'll never see a Dan who's not insane."

"Well, my investors wouldn't agree with you there."

"Right. I forgot about your investors." Abner shook his head and sorted through some invoices. Whenever Dan arrived late for work, which was often, he would claim he'd been meeting with some men who wanted to finance his venture. But Abner considered these alleged investors the most unbelievable part of the whole crazy scheme. He could accept many things, any number of alternate explanations for certain occurrences, but not these investors. The idea was too ludicrous. He'd finally decided Dan was simply one of those people who are chronically late for work.

But today Dan wouldn't drop the subject. "You don't believe me, do you?"

With his eyes skimming the papers, Abner replied, "Is it my subtle manner that gives me away?" Dan laughed and Abner looked up. "Well, I just can't believe anyone smart enough to be that rich could be so dumb. It's no secret the Russians censor everything. This movie will be so restricted it won't be yours at all."

"There you're wrong. It'll be partially mine, and that's ok by me."

"But that's censorship."

"Abner," he said patiently, "you're looking at it the wrong way. Think of it as a collaboration, as...as a mutually shared, visual illusion. That's what all movies are. The studios here do the same thing. You know what Universal's idea of a good movie is? It's one that makes a lot of money. The only difference between East and West is the motivating spirit."

"But it's evil. It's immoral."

Dan raised his hands in supplication. "I'm supposed to take 'immoral' from a man who hides *The Smurfs* from little children?" Abner started to protest, but Dan put his arm out to stop him. "So what'll it be today?" he asked, referring to the array of movies they played on the VCR while they worked. "What do you say we start with a little James Bond—*Dr. No*, perhaps—then take a trip back in time with, say, *Golddiggers of 33*, and finish up with *The Natural*?"

"Oh, you know, I was thinking we hadn't seen *Kramer vs. Kramer* for awhile."

"Too heavy. Good things are coming. We need something light."

"Ok. Trade the *Golddiggers* for *Heaven Can Wait*, and we have a deal."

"My friend, the essence of a happy life is compromise. Abner," he said with a flourish, "flip on the tube."

After Abner locked up the store that night, he climbed the two blocks to his small third floor apartment. Mr. Holmes nuzzled his shin as soon as he pushed through the door. Mr. Holmes was his cat. Abner had never owned a pet until two years ago when this reddish-brown and white calico began stalking him. For the next two weeks he tried everything he could think of to elude the cat, but he was unsuccessful. Wherever he dropped it off, whatever tricks he tried, the cat always found its way back to Abner's door. Eventually he gave up and they adopted one another.

"Yes, good evening, Mr. Holmes. Let's see what's for dinner." As he reached down to scratch the cat behind its ears, the animal shot off towards the kitchen. Abner shook his head and tossed a cassette onto a sofa covered with old newspapers and magazines. A frayed green blanket lay in a heap on the floor. The living room walls were decorated with movie posters: Bogart leading Hepburn down a jungle river in *The African Queen*; Dustin Hoffman staring blankly at Anne Bancroft's stockinged leg in *The Graduate*. A glitzy *Star Wars* poster hung in the tiny hall outside the bathroom. He tucked the entertainment section of the day's newspaper under his arm and went into the kitchen.

As soon as he entered the kitchen, he turned on the radio. An old refrigerator, pale and stocky like Abner, dominated the room. Encased in ice in the freezer he found six burritos, a Stouffer's lasagna, three beef and two chicken pot pies. I'm a true citizen of the world, he thought. The lower refrigerator compartment was almost bare. He removed some cat food, took out a beer, then opened the freezer again. He considered for a moment, then chiseled out a chicken pot pie.

After he slid the pie into the oven and fixed Mr. Holmes' supper, he leaned against the counter and opened the paper. He shuffled through the pages, but felt distracted. What if Dan really had some investors? Who could they be? Perhaps he was laundering money for the mob or some Latin American drug dealer. He pictured a short, wiry man with cocoa colored skin. He had a razor thin mustache and slicked back hair and a gold tooth that gleamed when he flashed his vicious smile. Abner shook his head. No, that didn't seem like Dan. Maybe this movie scheme was a tax shelter for a few Texas oil barons. Or maybe Dan was a flimflam man conning some poor, hard working souls out of their savings. No. Those possibilities didn't feel right, either. Well, maybe a studio had hired him. Maybe Universal wanted to make a movie of him making a movie. The multiplicity of this illusion appealed to Abner. It reminded him of a recent Brian DePalma movie, but it seemed awfully farfetched. Abner retreated full circle: Dan had no investors at all. He simply couldn't get out of bed in the morning.

When the buzzer on the stove announced his dinner was ready, Abner put on his pair of mitten pot holders. He opened the oven door and felt the rush of rising heat waves. He reached inside and as he lifted the pot pie the phone rang. Jesus, the phone hadn't rung in weeks. With the steaming pot pie in one mitten, he hopped over to the phone. He picked up the receiver with the other mitten and cradled it between collar bone and cheek, but just as he elbowed down the volume on the radio and said, "Hello?", the pie slipped out of his grasp to splatter onto the floor.

"'Hello? Mr. Abner? Are you alright?"

"Yes," he answered, slightly out of breath. "Actually, Abner is my first name, and I'm fine, thank you. I just had a little accident. I was fixing dinner and—"

"Mr. Abner, my name is Florence Jenson and I'm calling for the Veterans of Foreign Wars. Each year the V.F.W. sends a group of disabled veterans to a basketball game. We provide the men with a meal beforehand and a souvenir program at the game. The men seem to really enjoy it, and it costs you only ten dollars to sponsor a disabled veteran for this evening of entertainment. Do you think you would like to sponsor one or two of the men?" He envisioned a gray-haired woman in her bathrobe reading from a script. Mr. Holmes tentatively clawed the widening mound of pale yellow goo on the floor. "Mr. Abner?"

"Yeah...Sure. I suppose I could donate ten bucks." He couldn't unleash his disappointment on the vets. Abner watched Mr. Holmes edge towards a large floating chunk of chicken as Mrs. Jenson solicited the pertinent information. Looks like the night belongs to the cats and dogs of war, he thought.

When he hung up the phone he said, "Well Mr. Holmes, if you think we've switched meals and I'm eating your liver and bacon, you've got another think coming." He shoved a beef pot pie into the oven, and nudged the cat away from the congealing mess. On his knees cleaning up the floor he decided the black linoleum wasn't too bad: it was too dark to ever look dirty.

While he waited for his second supper he browsed through the TV section once more. "Oh yes," he mumbled, "That old Robert Redford spy flick. The one with Faye Dunaway." He had just decided to record the movie for his video collection when the buzzer on the stove went off again.

The next day Dan was later than usual. A long meeting with the investors, he explained when he finally arrived. "We're getting close."

"Sure," Abner nodded.

The store was empty. Dan leaned his spry frame against the back counter. The look in his deep set, blue eyes as he peered over his coffee cup reminded Abner it was time for the day's lesson. "Abner Abnerovitch, today I'll tell you about Kirlian photography. In the early forties two Russian scientists, Valentina and Semyon Kirlian, developed a complicated process that involves taking pictures of objects that lie in high frequency electrical fields. The resulting photographs reveal an aura surrounding whatever's in the picture."

Abner looked at him suspiciously. "An aura?"

"Yes, an aura. It's a sort of energy field that surrounds living things. Now here's the interesting part. Kirlian image patterns vary as the subject's emotional state changes. For instance, suppose I take a plant and develop a Kirlian picture of its aura. Then if I go back and pluck off a few leaves and take another picture, I'll find a completely different aura."

"So plants have feelings? Is that what you're saying? Plants have an emotional response you can measure?"

"Right, right. So listen: this stuff really intrigued me. I started thinking, if

57

plants can perceive pain, maybe they have some sense of aesthetics. After all, that's just a different type of integration and response to sensation. And then I thought about a TV set. It receives and emits electrical signals. So I decided to do this experiment. I took my begonia and put her right next to the TV. Then I played some movies and measured stuff like leaf span and soil pH, that kind of thing." His voice slipped into an excited hush. "And I think I'm onto something. She loves the Marx brothers. Five leaves grew a total three and 1/4 millimeters after *Duck Soup*. Then I showed her three Meryl Streep films, and she started wilting so much I had to water her constantly. And after a double feature of Charlton Heston she almost died. I really thought I'd lost her that time."

A young couple entered the store. Abner glanced at them, thinking this begonia charade was even more unbelievable than the mythical investors. Dan must think he was incredibly gullible. He smirked and said condescendingly, "Well, Charlton Heston would do that to anybody."

Abner turned back to the couple. The man was in his late twenties. He wore tight jeans, and where his shirt was open at the neck, Abner could see a thin gold chain resting on a mat of chest hair. His companion was slender with a model's high cheek bones, long auburn hair and steamy black eyes. Abner was slightly envious of the way she kept stroking the man's shoulder, running her fingers down his arm. The man was looking at the Science Fiction films: *Star Trek*, *Alien*, *The Empire Strikes Back*. Abner was about to boldly suggest the remake of *Invasion of the Body Snatchers*, when the woman straightened onto her tiptoes and whispered into the man's ear.

"Yeah?" he asked. She nodded and kissed him on the cheek. They walked over to the book with the listings of adult films. After they had turned a few pages, the man asked Dan, "Is *The Ecstasy Girls* in?"

"You got it." Dan said, then he looked at the woman and grinned. "How's it flyin', Caroline?"

She giggled, "Hi, Danny." Dan gave them the cassette, and arm-in-arm they hurried out of the store.

Abner pursed his lips and mimicked, "'Hi Danny.' You know her?"

"Sure. She's been in here before."

"No kidding. I wonder why I've never seen her? Well, somebody's going to have a fun afternoon."

Dan laughed, "You're damn right about that. And I'll tell you a little secret, pal. That fellow she's with isn't the one I saw her with last time." Abner stared at the empty doorway, and shook his head. He was continuously amazed at the curves in some peoples' lives.

He didn't notice what time Dan left the store. He'd been watching two acne-scarred teenage boys in torn sweatshirts root through the martial arts films. He vaguely recalled the phone ringing and Dan taking the call in the back. After arguing over which films to take the boys had settled on *Bruce Lee Meets the Dragon* and *Fists of Fury*. When they had left, Abner realized he was alone in the store.

"Well, ain't that great," he mumbled to himself. "I suppose he'll be back soon." But Dan didn't come back that afternoon, and he didn't show up the next day, or the one after that. Abner was about to call Mr. Field and ask him to send a replacement, but that afternoon Dan called.

"It's all set," he told Abner. "I leave for Russia tomorrow."

"Tomorrow?" Abner cried in disbelief.

"Yeah. That's why I haven't been in. I've been packing and getting my things together. Sorry I haven't called, but I was thinking of you. You know, I have a pretty good movie collection, and well, I don't know when I'll be back. You want to come over tonight and pick some out?"

"Gee Dan, I don't know. I mean it's awfully generous of you, but...."

"Come on. I feel I owe you something for the last few days, and anyway, who knows when I'll want them. Come over after work and take what you like."

That night Abner closed the store fifteen minutes early. He'd never been to Dan's apartment, and Dan seemed surprised to see him at the door. Dan had been so busy he'd forgotten about their phone call. "Come on in," he hollered as he retreated into his bedroom. "Take a look around and make yourself at home. Sorry the place is such a mess." Next to the television and the plant, Abner found a stack of tapes. He ran his finger across the titles as he looked around the apartment. Boxes filled with dishes and others packed with books on Russia were strewn across the living room. In a corner two crates stamped, "FRAGILE: VIDEO EQUIPMENT" leaned against one another. Bare spots on the wall unmasked where pictures once had hung. In the kitchen Abner saw a small samovar on the counter, but he couldn't tell if it worked or was just for show.

"Where's all this stuff going?"

Dan called out from the bedroom, "I've got an uncle with a warehouse cross-town. It's so big he'll never know the difference." He looked up to find

Abner watching him cram a suitcase full of toilet paper. "Got to be prepared for all emergencies," he laughed.

Abner smiled and looked back at the tapes. There were a good number of them that were difficult to find. He remembered Dan said he could take what he wanted, but he felt guilty, a bit overeager. He said, "You know, I never thought I'd live to see this. You going off to Russia and everything. And just like you planned it, too. I never figured you'd get the visas and permission. Or the money. Boy, I was sure you'd never get that money."

Dan put down his suitcase, and studied Abner. He opened his mouth but halted. Finally, he spoke, "You've got to go for it Abner. If watching movies is your thing, fine—watch movies. But I'm going to make mine."

"Yeah, but it still bothers me that you're working with the Russians."

Dan paused again before he said, "I'm interested in images, in the visual Russia. I want to show how they dress for the cold. I don't give a shit for politics." Then he put down his suitcase and crossed into the living room. He pulled *Chinatown* out of the stack of tapes, and slipped it into the VCR. On the television, Jack Nicholson was in handcuffs, vehemently protesting to a policeman. "Is this great or is this great?"

"Oh, it's definitely a classic, although I think Faye Dunaway overacts in parts."

Dan went on, "You remember the ending here? Nicholson tries to stop the cops from screwing up, but he's lied to them so much, they won't believe him. And since they won't listen to him, Faye Dunaway gets shot and the old man gets the girl." On the screen a crowd had gathered around the car where Faye Dunaway's body was slumped over the wheel. The car horn blared. Then Nicholson's partner led him back, led him away from the car and the body. "This is it, my favorite line." Dan cranked up the volume and recited with Nicholson's crony, "'Forget it, Jake. It's Chinatown'." The camera drew back into a long crowd shot and the lazy trumpet theme grew louder, very loud, as the credits began. Abner reached for the volume control, but Dan grabbed his hand and stopped him. Dan put a finger to his lips, and then with a pen he scrawled on a scrap of paper:

CIA

Abner started to laugh, but when he saw Dan's stern look, he gasped. The color drained from Abner's face. He tried to speak, but Dan waved him silent, gesturing vaguely at the walls around them. Hidden microphones, he implied. A bewildering multitude of theories scuttled across Abner's mind. Whose microphones, he wondered. Soviet? American? Did it matter? He'd seen enough spy movies to know either one was likely. Then he thought Dan must be joking. There was no way Dan was in the CIA. Abner said nothing but pointed to Dan and mouthed the word, "You?"

Dan returned his stare with a look of sanguine amusement. He shrugged as if to say, "Why not?" Then he turned down the volume on the television, and in a normal voice he asked, "So what tapes do you want? Oh Christ, why don't you just take them all. It'll be that much easier for me."

"You...you're sure?"

"Why not? It'll be our secret." He answered as he crumpled up the paper and pushed it deep into his pocket.

Abner murmured, "Ok."

"Oh, and one other thing. Would you take the begonia off my hands? I really don't have anyone else to give it to." Abner's eyes found the plant next to the television set. Knots of thick healthy stems gave off pale green shoots that were crowned with slick heart-shaped leaves. So many surprises, Abner thought, so many surprises. Just when you think you've considered all the possibilities, there's always one more.

They quickly filled a carton with tapes, and as soon as Abner had surrounded the plant with one arm, Dan shoved the overflowing carton of tapes under the other. Dan strode purposefully to the door, opened it, and tapped his foot while he waited for the overburdened Abner to plod across the room. Abner understood it was time to go; after all, Dan had a long night of packing before him.

When he stood outside the open doorway, Abner hesitated, "Does she, does she like Jack Nicholson?"

"Loves him." Dan looked at the begonia. "So long, Begonia." And then to Abner, "Remember, no Charlton Heston."

Abner studied the plant. "Right," he said, "No Charlton Heston." But Dan had already shut the door.

He stood in the hallway, filled with uncertainty. He looked around, but the empty hall was quiet. He shrugged, pulled the tapes and the plant closer to his body, and as he began descending the stairs, he whispered to the begonia, "How about if we watch a little Woody Allen? Is that ok? Maybe we'll start with one of the earlier, funny ones."

GUERRILLA LOVE

27 December, 18:32 hours: From his Mustang parked five houses away, Brown watches the van. A swirling light snow dusts the streets, but Brown is impervious to the chill. His chest blazes with anticipation. Inside their home the Collins are probably eating dinner. He imagines Collins charging two-fisted through a casserole and scoops of mashed potatoes, washing down white bread with noisy gulps of beer. Theresa sits patiently across from him, not hungry, sipping red wine. A car skitters past the Mustang, its headlights glazing the letters etched across the van: Collins' Heating & Plumbing. Service 24 Hours-A-Day.

Though he's been waiting for over an hour, Brown hasn't lost hope. He's invested too much time and effort to accept defeat this early. Tonight's family, the Cranstons, live in northern Cherry Hill, and with traffic only creeping in this snow, Collins can't possibly drive that far in less than thirty, forty minutes. He'll need another hour to repair the furnace, and then there's the icy ride home. Brown lifts the can of Bud tucked between his thighs and takes a swig. That leaves plenty of time, he thinks. If they call Collins.

After ten days of scouting the Cranston household, Brown has pinned down their routine. He knows what time Joe and Sharon leave for work, where the woman who keeps Chelsea (age sixteen months) lives, how Joe slips by The Red Oak at 6:15 every night and drinks a vodka martini with some men from his office. Brown has located the cutoff valve to their water line, marked the precise spot on the sidewalk where three feet down their sewer line empties into city pipe, and in his trunk he carries the specs for their furnace. Desire has carried Brown beyond rapture, beyond anything he's known before. He's slipped past all the guards at the usual boundaries; since last summer he's been running reconnaissance, attacking in stealth. He's learned how to deftly crack a sewer line and three sure ways to plug a sink trap. He's taught himself the hieroglyphics of electrical charts so when he sabotages a Carrier heat-pump the damage is minimal and no one is hurt. Because he works smoothly his presence has never been detected—each mission is just another fragment in the natural disorder. And now he knows the dank crossings of pipes in Cherry Hill, Voorhees, Marlton and Pennsauken better than the insides of the Mercurys and Fords he sells meekly by day.

Go back to last June on a sweltering afternoon. Heat waves rise off the asphalt. Hydrangeas wilt in despair. Half drunk and restless, Brown grabs a shirt out of the laundry and wanders over to the mall. He sweeps in and out of stores, his muddy eyes skipping past the knots of shopping women. In the Radio Shack he's surprised to find his tired face staring at itself on a television screen. He studies that face for a minute: the thick lips, the stubbled jowls creased by years of solitude. With pudgy fingers he rearranges the unruly hair to hide the bald spot, then realizing it's hopeless he stops and frowns at the futility. Let's face it, he tells himself, it's not what you were hoping to see. He turns away from the camera, and as vulnerable as a marshmallow in a pinball machine, he plunges into the crowd.

"Those are very nice shoes, the best we carry. All the stitching is done by hand." He looks down to find himself slapping a shoe against his palm. He must have strayed into a shoe store. The woman continues, "Maybe I can find your size in the back." She tugs the shoe out of his hand so gently she might have been taking a toy from a toddler. Her fingernail slides lightly, almost accidentally, across his palm.

Startled by her touch, he turns to discover one of the most striking women he's ever seen. Her neck is as smooth as marble. Her face is fine boned and pale, except for the soft clouds of rouge painted high on her cheeks. "Your size?" she asks, her eyes resting lightly on his.

"10-C," he croaks.

"10-C," she purrs. "Please sit down." She nods to a seat, but he remains standing until the last flip of her skirt disappears into the back of the store. Then he settles into a chair facing the stacked rows of empty shoes. When she returns she kneels silently before him, and while her knowing fingers casually unlace and remove his old Florsheims, his eyes trace the slender curve of her legs to where the black silk straddles, then modestly dips, between her thighs. The frilly edge of her black slip peeks down and wraps itself around his heart, squeezing a burst of desire into his throat. He swallows, strengthens his grip on the chair while her small hands cradle his sole. Finally, she slides his foot into the shoe. It fits as snugly as a dagger in its sheath. What grace she has. His anguish flares.

Still admiring the shoes, she snakes her tongue along the moist line of lipstick, then cocks her head at him. "Aren't they marvelous?"

"For new shoes they sure are comfortable."

"You won't find anything better. That's the finest Italian leather you can buy. Some men say they're too expensive. They tell me, 'Theresa, three hundred dollars is too much for a pair of shoes.' But they're short sighted. They're tiny men with tiny visions of the world. You know, a man says a lot with his shoes."

"How's that?"

"Look around you." She flicks a disdainful wrist at the mall. "Show me a man with scruffy old shoes and I'll show you a man who's lost his bearings. He's unsure of himself. A woman sees these things. She knows how to read them, how to use them. You wear a nice pair of shoes and you tell the world you know who you are."

"Oh, so it's an image thing."

"Oh no, it's much more than that. You make it sound too superficial. Think of it as a glimpse into the inner person, a revelation of his microcosm."

Brown smiles at her. For the first time since awakening that morning the ache behind his eyes is gone. "You know, I've got to say, I've never had a conversation like this in a shoe store." He looks at the empty shoes in front of them, then back to her. "It's strange, but after just a few minutes of listening to you, I can tell that you're different from most people. You seem to be a person who makes simple things look complicated and complicated things look simple. Am I right?" She shrugs her shoulders ambiguously. "So what time do you get out of here?" The question has tumbled out on its own, before he'd even formed the thought, and his face grows hot and flushed with embarrassment as he waits for her rejection. Never in his life has Brown picked up a salesgirl.

Curious, she studies him as she tucks a loose strand of hair behind one ear. He lowers his eyes until he hears her whisper in a voice ripe with promise, "Meet me in the coffee shop next to Penney's at four."

"At four," he echoes in hollow astonishment.

Her smile is a string of white pearls. "Now, will that be cash or charge?"

At 4:15 Brown sits alone behind a lemonade, sketching a Mercury Cougar on a napkin. A box of new shoes lies beside him on the floor. Fooled again, he murmurs, unable to forget the impression of her fingers pressed upon his toes. He drops his head into his hands as sleek young bodies shimmer across his mind. Forty-two years alone and I can still be found. He remembers a magical sultry night, the evening of his brother's wedding. After hours of celebration, the maid of honor had guided Brown to the deserted hotel pool. "This way, Brown," she teased. "This way." Giddy with champagne and fresh love, they lingered in the water past the first scarlet rays of light, but in the afternoon she flew home to Michigan and was lost to him forever. That was fifteen years ago and since that night whole lives have passed, galaxies have died, but Brown cannot shake his furies, the swift murmurings of desired voices. "This way, Brown. This way." Never again has he ridden that pulse of unconscious delirium, and now all he wants is silence, a truce. He longs to steal past desire, to be immune from whatever anguish might yet be twisted from his shriveled heart. But just last night, through thin apartment walls, merciless dawn taunted him with a girl's salacious laughter.

"Sorry I'm late," she says, sliding into the booth. A surge of relief washes over him. "A customer couldn't make up his mind. It took him twenty minutes to figure out he wanted Hushpuppies instead of Wallabees. Honestly, some fools think I have nothing better to do than talk about cheap shoes. May I?" She reaches for the lemonade.

He pushes the glass across the table, wondering if she'd held that customer's foot the same way she'd held his. "But you must get a lot of people wandering in who don't know what they want." She nods vigorously, her lips pursed around the straw. "I guess you don't like selling shoes?"

"Do you like selling Fords?"

"What? How the hell—"

"Your pen."

He looks down at it. "Bob Ross Ford" is engraved on the side. "A guess?" Her sly grin reveals nothing. He protests, "But I could be a mechanic, or an accountant...or, or maybe I took the damn thing from my brother-in-law."

"But you didn't." She sets down the glass in the middle of the table.

With one hand stroking his chin he scrutinizes her. "Don't take this the wrong way, but you're not like any woman I ever met who worked selling shoes."

"I'll take that as a compliment."

"So how'd you end up there? I mean, a woman like you...it seems you could be doing lots of different things."

She lifts the straw and twirls it with her fingers. "What do you mean, 'a woman like you'?"

"I don't know. You just seem different. Like when we were in the store and you were talking about men and their shoes, it seemed like you could see inside people. You could tell right away what they're about, what's scratching underneath their skins."

"And what's scratching underneath your skin?"

"I'm wondering why you work in a shoe store."

"Oh," she snorts. "That's easy. When I moved from San Francisco I needed the money and it was the only job I could find. People don't trust...they're not very enlightened here."

"Why'd you move in the first place?"

"I'm afraid my excuse for moving is the same dumb one most people have. Misguided love."

"Is there another kind? I swore off it years ago. But you're still wearing somebody's diamond."

She looks down at her hand and says wistfully, "It's not that simple, Mr. Brown. Not for me."

"Just 'Brown,' no 'Mister.'" She smiles back at him. "But why do you stay if you don't love him?"

"Why do you sell Fords?"

He laughs, "You got me. Anyway, it's been so long since I made a sale, my last customer bought one with tail fins."

"Oh no. I'm sure you're a marvelous salesman."

He casually reaches for the lemonade, but she intercepts his hand and locks it between hers. She rubs her palms hard across its ridges and knuckles, runs her sharp nails inside the creases of his palm. The light that danced in her black eyes dissolves as she stares at him. He breaks out in a sweat. Finally, in a low voice she says, "Brown, I can also tell a lot from a man's hand."

"Oh...How do you mean?" For another long uncertain minute she continues to massage his hand. Something has slipped out of control here and he feels foolishly exposed. Whatever this is, it doesn't happen in the coffee shop next to Penney's.

"Like his shoes, a man's hands tell a story. The calluses, the web of lines on the palm, the shape of the fingernail, the bend in the joints."

"And mine?"

She clasps his fingers tighter. "Brown, are you familiar with the Yin-Yang symbol? Do you know it?"

"Those two little fishes curled around each other?"

"Into a circle. Yes, that's the one. It's the union of opposites into the whole. You and I, Brown?" she whispers, raising an eyebrow. "Will you come to me tonight?" He glances nervously at her diamond. "It's all right. You must trust me." She slowly releases his hand, dragging three long nails across his skin. Numbed, he watches a thin line of blood rise along his palm while she writes her address on the napkin.

"Nine o'clock," she tells him as she stands.

He looks first to the flowery script on the napkin, then to her stern and knowing face. Already safe, he answers, "Wonderful."

In late September the dreams began. Brown awakens in a riotous sweat as the heart-pounding image of an electric plumbing snake whirling into his spine slowly fades. In the day while trying to sell an Escort or a Thunderbird he will suddenly picture them caught in the act: he arches his back in delirious orgasm just as an outraged plumber enters the room. A thick hand extends the business end of a monkey wrench that will smash past hair and skin through skull to brain. He began to dread sleep, his appetite turned sour. Brown has few friends, but he trusts a fellow salesman named Tom. A bear of a man with curly red hair and sleepy blue eyes, Tom could sell encyclopedias to the blind. So after revising his tale to reveal its immoral aspects but conceal its illegal ones, he invites Tom to join him at a bar one day after work. He tells him about the dreams.

Tom laughs, "So you're coming and going at the same time."

"Thanks, man. This is serious."

"Seriously, can you think of a better way to go?"

Brown considers various possibilities, then replies, "Well, I'd planned on a later departure."

"You're already dead," his friend answers flatly.

"What?"

"Look," Tom sets down his drink and hunches forward in the booth. "It's like getting a squeeze job in a Pinto going 80 down the turnpike. You see what I'm saying?" Brown shakes his head. "Ok. Think of it as your basic choice of transmissions. One guy wants an automatic, another takes a stick, but they're both transmissions. In your dream you die just as you're coming, right?"

Brown nods. "Death and orgasm are interchangeable here. I'm telling you, these dreams are the blossoms of your classic Freudian conflict. You got a death wish, pal. You're trying to desert your own lonely body." Satisfied, he leans back and takes a long draw on his beer.

Brown gapes at him. "You've read Freud?"

"Of course not," Tom answers with disgust and wipes his mouth with his sleeve.

It's a cold afternoon in mid November. Darkness will be coming soon. Brown sees the red chalk "X" on the manhole cover, and pulls the unmarked Bob Ross Ford van over to the curb. After turning off the ignition he takes several deep breaths, then climbs down from the cab. On the sidewalk he unfolds the map but he can't focus on it. He remains unsure, despite his equipment and elaborate disguise, that he will blend into the routine of the street, and his eyes keep darting about to see if anyone is watching. Finally, satisfied he is not regarded with suspicion, he puts the map away, pries off the manhole cover, surrounds the hole with four Day-Glo orange warning cones, and descends into the sewer. Plumbing work is easier in the fall. Soon the freezing weather will arrive, and he suspects the pipes will become be too cold and slippery, but then he can switch over to furnaces and heat pumps. Inside, the dark pipe is narrow, so narrow he must crawl on hands and knees. He's barely crawled fifty yards before a cramp stabs his lower back. He pauses to stretch the tight muscles, but then slogs onward. His schedule is strict; he has no time to rest. Out of the darkness before him trickles a foul smelling, black stream, and though his boots and coveralls are waterproof, the dampness always seeps through. When he undresses at home his skin will be a variegated mosaic of pale-edged grime stains.

As they lay under the sheets that first night Theresa revealed her rules to him. Her first explanation was simple, the obvious one: Brown sabotages the plumbing, then the victims—all reliable customers—call Collins, and with her husband out of the house, she and Brown can make love without fear of being caught. At first he thought she was kidding, playing some sort of bizarre joke on him, but when he understood she was serious, he said, "You must be crazy. There are easier ways for us to get together. You can come to my place. I live alone."

She took his face between her hands, locked fingers on his cheeks, and in a voice as soothing as a snake chant, she whispered, "Listen to me, Brown. Listen to me well. When I held your foot today, when my hands rubbed yours, I slipped in through the backdoor of your soul. And I understood. You awaken every morning searching for release and now you have found me. If you let me, I can lead you to the peace you crave. I am that woman, Brown." She stroked his cheek gently. "I can look into your eyes right now and see you know it, too."

"I...I don't understand. Why...?"

"What matters is quite simple. You must follow my instructions." His throat was so parched he could not speak. His face turned pale, his skin grew cold. Brown began shaking, shaking uncontrollably, as if some truth had whisked him to the verge of a seizure. He could ask no more.

Later that night in his apartment, he realized his choice was either to enlist in her underground or lose her, but by then it was too late. He had already journeyed past volition. Indeed, he had just completed the first part of his training: body and soul, he was committed to her, and after that first evening the ritual was established. As Brown dresses to leave, Theresa will pass him a folded sliver of paper with another name, address, date and time. In silence now, he accepts their agreement, never questioning her choices. He simply transforms those names and dates to fit the contours of a new paradigm: does her charge mean work above ground or below? Will he stalk furnace lines or sewers?

At a junction where the pipes became narrower, he slithers on elbows through the cramped darkness. The spasm in his back suddenly lunges to his shoulders, and he slips on a patch of slick grime, flopping into the water. The rough cement rips gashes in the resewn elbows and patched knees of his coveralls. He spits out the muck. Resting for a moment, he listens to the hollow sounds of the sewer: the tinkling water, the echo of his heavy breathing. He pulls out the well-creased map from his pocket, studies it by flashlight one last time, then looks at his watch: 16:20 hours. Precisely on schedule. From a heavy-duty tool box linked to his waist by a rope he removes an amorphous mound sealed in two plastic bags, a new compound he'd found two nights before in a hardware store. At home he'd tested it in smaller pipes, a model sewer he's constructed in his bathtub, and as promised by the people at DuPont, the putty turned hard the instant it came in contact with moisture. Elation had surged through his chest. He felt as if he'd graduated from fire crackers to TNT. But then he remembered standing with his purchase in the checkout line. The clerk, just making pleasant conversation, had reduced him to incoherent mumblings. Brown had not anticipated someone asking what he wanted to fix.

From the tool box he removes a pair of dry latex gloves, the kind housewives use for washing dishes, and slides them over the heavy wet ones he wears. He carefully unseals the two plastic bags, and in ten minutes he's occluded the pipe. Mission accomplished. He knows that in a matter of hours, Collins' revved-up Roto-Rooter will knock through his wall, but that is also part of the plan—he wants no one to follow his slimy path beneath the street. He hurries back to the manhole cover, his frosty breath coming faster, his heart racing. In his imagination a snarling policeman always stands waiting at the hole, tapping an impatient billy club against his thigh. He looks up. No one is there. Relieved, he climbs out of the sewer, removes the orange cones, and nonchalantly packs the equipment into the truck. He looks at his watch: 16:55 hours. Not bad, he thinks with pride, and rubbing his back, he imagines Theresa in her negligee, the black lace one she's promised to wear. With wanton smile and crooked finger she will beckon him to her bed tonight.

27 December, 20:27 hours: Brown raises the binoculars, scans the house, and frowns: they should have called by now. He no longer worries about being stopped in his car with shards of concrete, or large dead rodents, or strange tools a car salesman would never need. He only worries his victims won't call, or they'll endure the night and phone in the morning, or perhaps they'll call someone else. Then his efforts will have been wasted. It happened once. For three hours he sat huddled in his car on a surprisingly cold autumn night, abandoned, marooned. When he finally understood he had failed, he drove to a windowless bar on Admiral Wilson Boulevard where the dancers wore nothing but painted smiles. He rapidly tossed down three whiskeys, but the mocking laughter persisted. In grim desperation he saw only her face, and at last, when he could no longer stand it, he crept to the rear of the bar and purchased some joyless relief in a cell large enough to hold only a mattress and a redhead named Bambi.

He sets down the binoculars and thinks back, as he often does, to that first invitation to her house. How did she know her husband wouldn't be home? Had Collins told her in the morning he'd be working late? Did she wake up that day planning to take a lover? And are there others? Does she command a whole army of lovers who destroy pipes by day and make love to her by night? He is jealous of them all and he isn't even certain they exist. Many times he has come close to asking, but each time he backs away. He knows he wouldn't believe her answer.

Around Thanksgiving, he started shopping in Army Surplus stores, and since then he only feels comfortable wearing combat fatigues and a bandana. When he goes out on a venture he paints black crescents under his eyes. He has written on a paper he keeps pinned above his bed, "Red is the color of anarchy and love." He spends his free afternoons prowling through plumbing supply and hardware stores, searching for new ideas and better tools. He wants each action to be different, more subtle than the last. When he tells her the details of his labors, of his cunning designs, she seems pleased; it's another secret the lovers share. But recently, as he described the way he clogged a soil pipe and clipped the wires to a furnace, he found himself wondering if she was just pretending.

Over the past two months he's lost twenty-five pounds. He spends most of his time scouting and on the rare days when he appears in the showroom his mind is elsewhere. Only two weeks before, on the morning of a strike, he remembered he'd left his A. O. Smith water heater plans in his desk at the office. He scurried by to pick them up, completely forgetting he was dressed in his uniform. The next day Tom badgered him into having a drink after work.

"Brown, old buddy, you've got to pull yourself together. You're acting like somebody stripped your gears and oiled them with sand. No one remembers the last time you made a sale. People are talking. That was some stunt you pulled yesterday, wearing those combat clothes and camouflage makeup to work. You do that again, and Bob Ross is going to nail your ass. What in God's name were you thinking?"

"I thought it was Veteran's Day."

"I don't care if it's Halloween or Henry Ford's birthday, you better not screw up like that again." He swirled his drink, then softly added, "You know, Veteran's Day's in November."

"I was confused," he chuckled weakly.

"Brown, as much as it pains me to say it, you're turning into one sorry piece of shit. I've tried being sympathetic, but you're simply getting worse. Are you seeing anyone besides that crazy woman?"

"She's not crazy and no, I'm not." He was touched by Tom's concern, but he cared no more than Tom did, which is to say only a bit. They both knew

Brown wouldn't be selling cars much longer.

"At first I thought it was good you were getting out, even if she is married, but now I'm not so sure. I think this woman's poison for you. Maybe there's something to those crazy dreams you're having. Maybe it's a warning."

"Maybe I should do something?"

"Right." Tom was encouraged by his response. "Shift it into first and see how easy it is to get out of there."

"That's what I'll do. Get myself in gear." But even as he spoke he knew nothing could be changed.

27 December, 21:47 hours: Brown lights another Marlboro. When they were first in love he was pleased she smoked the same brand. In those early, less complicated days Theresa would lie with him after love and share the black plastic ash tray as it bobbed up and down on his chest. He thinks of her now every time he lights a cigarette, which is at least sixty times a day, but when he ruminates on this he knows that sixty falls short of the truth.

Once, after making love he had pulled her to him and whispered urgently, "Theresa, my love, you're priceless. You know that, right?"

She propped herself up on her elbows, and her tousled black hair cascaded around his face. "Now you understand. What a man receives for free he soon finds worthless. I give you so much more, my love, than you will ever know. All I ask for is a gesture, one small token." Then she lowered her face to his chest, weaved butterfly kisses down his flank, and together they made love once more.

Sometimes she babbles like a prophet, scattering a trail of shadowy riddles behind her. Sometimes she is a teacher. "Koan" is one word she's taught him, a word he's only recently begun to understand. Her lessons take him through such strange forms that the grotesque nature of his deeds no longer amazes him. He submits, awed by the scope of her knowledge, mesmerized by her powers, but he is no longer a novice. He has learned that power flows both ways, that she possesses a craving which complements his own. He's even caught glimpses of the connections between this power and their love. He pictures their love as fragments, as a jigsaw puzzle where the pieces of the outer frame lock together, but the center ones don't fit. There is a secret in the middle that is opaque, impenetrable. He knows he's crossed over, crossed into a madness he thinks of as a dank, narrow sewer pipe. Cramped and aching, he

72

crawls down the middle with a flashlight. Is he trudging deeper into the darkness, or is he heading instead for the manhole above? In an occasional lucid moment, he wonders if Theresa is in the pipe with him. Is she in front, leading him further into the darkness, or is she following from behind? Do their pipes run parallel and only seem to cross? Or maybe the pipe is one of her crazy Yin-Yang circles, and like dogs they only chase each other's tails.

The driveway light blinks on and Brown raises his binoculars. They are walking arm-in-arm to the van. The poor man is about his height, though thicker through the chest and shoulders, with squirrelly hair poking from underneath a woolen cap. Theresa is wrapped in a white silk robe. Jesus, she must be freezing, he thinks, but then he scowls. The robe is far too expensive for a plumber's wife. Is this dance, then, merely prostitution? He has constructed an elaborate, perverted chain where the currency for Theresa's charms is sabotage, and while Brown claims his pleasure, that laughing Collins, a knowing pimp, collects the money from his customers, all victims of the cold or broken pipes. This thought has nagged at Brown before, but each time he's shoved the intruder to the back of his mind. And yet....

Through his binoculars he sees the pouty angel's smile kiss her husband goodbye. She shivers as she waves at the plumber's van, which snorts, then rumbles out of the driveway and disappears down the street. Brown crushes his cigarette, sets the timer and switch, then hops out of his car. As he approaches her house he thinks how convenient it is that while the Cranstons use electric heat, the Collins have gas. He knows because that afternoon, while Collins fixed pipes and Theresa hawked loafers, he also raided the Collins home. Their basement furnace is now connected to his newest device, one sure to impress. By remote control he can override the valves on their furnace. The first switch blocks the flow, extinguishing both pilot and flame. Then a timer triggering another valve will release gas at a tremendous rate. Everything is set, and if his calculations are right—and they haven't failed him yet—she'll be too distracted to notice any smell while they make love in the second floor den. He will light his usual after-love cigarette and the outstretched fist of a coppery fireball will flail this house against the sky.

In the cold white silence he climbs the steps to her porch. She opens the door before he can knock. She was never one to care what spying neighbors might think. She embraces him, flashes her hot tongue in his ear, and whispers—and at last he is assured that she whispers to him only—"Oh, my darling."

ONE DAY'S WORK

By all accounts, the job should have been an easy one. The design called for an unadorned structure to be built down the path from the estate house. The single, paneled room with the modest exterior siding would be an artist's studio. First Virginia was the general contractor, and they had sent in a bulldozer and backhoe which cleared out the scrub, finished the grading, and scooped out the trenches. Max worked for the concrete man. All he had to do was to make sure the ground was dry, then direct his crew in pouring the footings and inserting the steel anchor bolts before the concrete could harden. That was it. His boss had given him this job because it was Max's first as a foreman and also because the boss didn't have any choice: he'd just fired the old foreman for drinking and insubordination.

Like most of the men, Max had started off raking out the thick grey mounds which oozed down the mixer. For months he'd worked in a mindless rhythm until the day the planer showed up too drunk to work. The boss had handed Max the trowel, and at the end of the afternoon, when Max looked over the smooth surface he'd tamped out of the lumps and pocks of concrete, he felt a rush of pride. He wielded that trowel for the next five years, and might have continued for several more but even his simple life wasn't that simple. He'd married and his wife was still in school. Even though Sarah worked, they found it increasingly difficult to complete the link between paychecks, and so when his predecessor was fired, Max didn't hesitate to accept the promotion.

He arrived at the site thirty minutes early, and inspected the cleared ground, then inspected it again, but the studio was so small this only took fifteen minutes. Then he began to worry his men would be late. He knew the unpredictability of laborers on a Monday morning, and was quite relieved when at ten past seven the truck and two cars lumbered down the driveway. After the usual cups of coffee and shuffling around, the pouring began. The September sun lifted above the surrounding wood and its warmth gave Max confidence. They would be rinsing left-over sludge out of the mixer by mid-afternoon.

Because the churning mixer was loud, Max didn't hear the Buick roll across the driveway or the crisp slam of its front door. The unexpected tap on his shoulder startled him, and when he jerked around he was further surprised to find himself confronted by a fleshy old face bristling with anger. Max motioned to the driver to turn off the mixer.

The old man was waving his arms, but in the sudden silence, his frenzy seemed ridiculous. He shouted at Max, "What the fuck is going on here?"

"We're pouring the footings. You aren't the inspector, are you?"

The man's flabby cheeks reddened, and he stomped past Max towards the trenches. The workmen, quick to grab any chance to stop working, stepped back and leaned against their rakes. They watched the old man with curious, bemused smiles as he waddled across the site. Twice he stopped beside an oak whose bark had been gouged by a backhoe. He ran his palm across the gash and shook his head, but he said nothing until he approached Max again. "Would it be possible for you to explain why you're digging these strange canals? Is it a ritual of some sort? For your sake, I hope this isn't a fraternity prank, because Dean Williams is a friend of mine and—"

"Just who the hell are you, anyway?" Max interrupted.

"Who am I? Who am I? I am Fitzburke Kelly, and this land, which for some reason you have seen fit to desecrate, belongs to me. The real question is, who the fuck are you?"

Max squinted and rubbed his chin. "Well, I'm Maxwell Scott. We're from Chester's Concrete, the concrete sub for your studio."

"Studio? What studio? No one's building a studio here. Now get those men and that cement bucket of yours and leave this place instantly." He snapped his wrists at the mixer.

"Now just a second. I'm sure there's a contract. I've got the blueprints in the truck, if you want to see them. Chester was going over them yesterday with the super from First Virginia and that Mr. Blumkey—"

"Blumkey. Of course. I should have recognized his oily smell immediately. I felt a twinge when he was asking for that power-of-attorney, but that creamy voice of his always coats my better judgement. 'Two months you'll be in Europe, traveling with this once-in-a-lifetime, masterpiece exhibit. You want I should bother you if a pipe breaks or the roof springs a leak?' He must have planned this from the start. That bastard is always trying to do my thinking for me." Kelly's anger had dissipated over the course of his explanation, and he concluded in an offhand tone, "Go on, just get that machine out of here as quickly as you can." He turned and walked towards the front porch.

"Oh shit," Max muttered. The concrete was already mixed and if it wasn't poured soon, it would harden. He knew what Chester would think if he returned with a truck half full of concrete. He scrambled up the walk after the painter. "There's no reason to be so hasty here, Mr. Kelly. If you don't want to use it as a studio, the building would make a fine guest house, or even a rec room. I bet you could even change it into a greenhouse, if you rearrange the windows a little."

Kelly stepped up to Max. His puffy lids narrowed his eyes to slits. "Let me explain this once more. I don't give a rat's ass about your blueprints or your contracts. I certainly don't need a rec room. So leave, before you're sorry that you didn't."

One of the workers in the truck shouted out, "What you gonna do old man? Run us off with some itty-bitty paint brush?"

Max waved the man silent, but he couldn't think of any route to reconciliation. On his first day as foreman he certainly didn't want to back down in front of his men. He also knew how Chester would react, and yet, he felt Kelly was somehow right. He was staring at Kelly, not knowing what else to do, when suddenly the old man turned and marched up to the house. Max watched him and sighed, thinking the painter had given in.

From inside the truck a man called out to Max, "What a fucking chump."

Max shrugged. "From what Chester says, that fucking chump makes more money from one picture than you do in six months."

"That don't keep him from being a chump."

The men laughed, and slowly drifted back to work. They had been pouring for another ten minutes when Kelly threw open the door and raised the nozzle of a hose. They'd barely seen him, barely had time to recognize the hose for what it was, when Kelly discharged a torrent of paint. Waves of shocking pink doused Max and the men, splattered and smeared thick globs across their cars and the mixer. The men jumped, they shouted curses and knocked into one other as they tried to dodge the shower of paint, but the tight faced, old man kept on spraying. He tracked down each one until all were so drenched and embarrassed they could only retreat, their caravan bleeding a shocking pink trail down the highway.

In his new office Max changed clothes. Despite his embarrassment, he still believed Kelly was justified in his view, and this notion embarrassed Max even more. Something must be lacking in a man who emerged sympathetic rather than angry after an involuntary baptism in paint. His thoughts were disrupted by the phone ringing. It was Rose, Chester's secretary.

"Max, I just found a note here from Chester saying he wants to meet you in the warehouse at two o'clock sharp."

Max looked at his watch. "Two o'clock sharp was forty-five minutes ago."

"I just got back from lunch."

"Is that what I'm supposed to tell Chester?"

"I really don't care what you tell him," she said and hung up the phone.

Max left his office and crossed the wide work yard, kicking the loose gravel and sidestepping the water filled ruts that tires had dug into the clay. He felt the day pressing in on him, discerning in this something murky but loud, a menace feeding on itself and growing stronger. He paused at the warehouse entrance, letting his eyes adjust to the absence of sunlight. The warehouse was the size of an airplane hangar, filled with huge mounds of sand and long rows of sacks of cement heaped onto coarse wooden pallets. Chester was talking to a man on a forklift. His white shirt billowed loose as his hand waved a cigar. When the man on the forklift saw Max he nodded to him. Chester abruptly stopped talking and charged towards Max, tapping a scolding finger against the face of his wristwatch. As he crossed the warehouse Chester's arm grazed against a stack of cement bags. He was always doing that, bumping against things. People, walls, furniture. It reminded Max of the way football players butt shoulders along the sidelines before a game, except he was sure Chester wasn't conscious of it.

Chester extended his arm, and with an air of concern he asked what had happened. Max told him the story and Chester replied, "I'm sure you can get him to change his mind."

"Well, I don't know. He seemed pretty serious."

Chester glanced at the pink splotches on Max's cheek, "That kind of thinking won't solve the problem. You've got to complete our end of this contract. This job is one day's work and nothing more."

"But it's his property, his money."

Chester grasped both of Max's shoulders. Cigar fumes engulfed them. "Max, I can see where you're coming from, and to be fair, maybe there's a point to what you're saying, but I've got to tell you, your approach to the situation leaves me a little concerned about your loyalties. I mean, here I am, willing to overlook a mixer full of useless concrete, willing to overlook a punk paint job on the side of my best truck, and you can't see to take my side? What would you think?" Max started to protest but Chester released his grip and waved him silent. "Let me put this job into perspective for you. Chester's Cement and Concrete is a small operation. I'm no giant, no corporate barracuda, and so when First Virginia comes to me and says, 'Hey Chester, how'd you like to do the concrete on our thirty-two million dollar Southland Project?', I'm grateful. I appreciate the consideration. And when they return a few weeks later to ask for a little assistance on a dumb little studio, I'm more than happy to oblige. Max, you've been in the business long enough to know I'm making next to nothing on this job, but I'm a man who understands gratitude. Are you with me so far?"

Max nodded.

"Good." Chester squeezed Max's shoulder again. "Now let's say I'm the head honcho at First Virginia and I find out Chester can't finish this one simple studio. I might start having second thoughts. I might start thinking he's not the best man for my Southland team. Max, we want to stay on the Southland team. We need to stay on the Southland team. People could lose their jobs if we don't stay on the Southland team."

"But what if we explained it to First Virginia? Like you said, it's such a small job. What's it to them?"

"It's the name. This Kelly guy is a famous artist. His paintings sell all across Greenwich Village. We're talking prestige here, Max. When that CEO at First Virginia thinks of this job, he doesn't see a little studio. No, he sees a glossy ad with Fitzburke Kelly and First Virginia spread across two pages of *Today's Builder*, and it gives the guy a hardon."

"So you want me to talk to Kelly."

"Now you're catching on."

"But what can I say?"

"Get to know the man. Find out where his handles are, then twist them open. You're in management now. Let him know you mean business." He squeezed Max's shoulder once more, oblivious to the ashes which tumbled down Max's sleeve. "You understand how much this means to us?"

Max met Chester's firm eyes and he nodded once more. He left the warehouse with a hollow feeling inside, and decided to go home. As he drove between the work yard gates he waved to his crew who were smoking cigarettes in a loose huddle near the truck. They remained still, responding with the glassy stares of men who plan to disappear just after payday.

When Max arrived home the house was empty. He'd hoped Sarah wouldn't be working that night, but the kitchen calendar had a 'W' penciled in for the day. He spent a long time scrubbing in the shower, then ate his dinner in front of the television. Afterwards he stretched out on the couch and fell asleep. When he awakened, Sarah still wasn't home. Jim and Tammy Bakker were talking to Ted Koppel. Max watched for a while, then turned off the television and went upstairs.

Max usually slept soundly, but that night he awoke well before dawn. He worked on relaxing back into sleep, and eventually succeeded; but his wakening thoughts had already snared Kelly and carried him into his dream. Their motorboat was stranded in the middle of the river. Something was wrong with the engine. Across the flinty, gray green water Max saw Kelly's house perched high on the bank, but the distance was too far to swim. Before he could even cross halfway, the rain promised by the wind and dark, fat clouds would overtake him. Unsure what to do, Max clung to the windshield and watched Kelly pull off the stalled engine's casing and punch the choke with the handle of a paint brush. Kelly rammed the engine over and over, his blows growing fiercer, his aim less precise. Suddenly, the river spat a frothy whitecap over the rail, and a loose wrench rapped Max across the throat. Through breathless pain he tried yelling to the old man, "Did you squeeze the fuel pump? Did you squeeze the fuel pump? Did you squeeze the fuel pump?"

He awakened with a mouth full of pillow. Beside him, Sarah lay twisted in the sheets. Max exhaled the pillow and straggled from the bed towards the bathroom, nearly tripping over the pile her waitress' uniform made in the center of the floor. After he'd washed, he fixed his breakfast, a bowl of cereal crowned with banana slices, and a glass of juice. As he ate he skimmed through one of the textbooks she'd left on the kitchen table, *Information Processing in the Computer Age*. He tried reading in a few different places, but each time the sentences slipped into an indecipherable jargon, so he flipped through the pages and looked at the strangely labeled diagrams of gray boxes connected by black arrows. He'd almost finished eating when Sarah came downstairs. She half filled a mug with coffee, pulled open the refrigerator and poured in an equal amount of cream. She took a long swallow, and when she lowered the cup and pulled back the tangled chestnut hair which hid her face, their eyes met for the first time that day. A faint white mustache colored her upper lip.

She turned her face to the window to see if the neighbor's paper had arrived and dabbed her mouth with a napkin. She said, "I got a call from the bursar's office yesterday. My tuition's overdue."

"I thought you told me you'd paid it."

"You said you'd sent the check."

"I don't remember saying that."

"So already that makes two things you've forgotten." She announced it flatly, as if she were reporting the weather or the color of a passing car.

He ate a few more bites of cereal and finished his juice. It was time for a reset. "You missed Jim and Tammy on Ted Koppel last night. It was incredible. Some people have no shame."

"That Tammy looks so sleazy."

"And his smile. Did you ever see a smile so insincere?"

"Unctuous, that's my word for Jim Bakker. It's that forehead of his. No one with a forehead that wide could be anything but unctuous. And yet people send them millions of dollars. Maybe we should start our own church. I'll quit school, we'll quit our jobs, and—"

"I may not have to worry about quitting mine." He told her about the confrontation with Kelly and Chester's ultimatum.

She said, "Chester should get a lawyer and sue."

"Sue Kelly?"

"Damn right. Sue Kelly, sue the agent, sue the architect. Sue the neighbors who live next door. I know some lawyers, guys who eat at my station every night, and they'd snatch up a case like this faster than you can say ipso facto loco."

"That's nice, but even Chester can't afford the kind of money they'd charge."

She lapped up his ignorance. "You just don't know, do you? Lawyers take these cases on a contingency basis." Her tongue played with the words. "That's the way these things work."

On a contingency basis. He shook his head, picturing the slick lawyers she'd been listening to.

He drove southeast, the same route he'd taken the day before, driving past the nests of shopping plazas, past the unplowed fields of the Southland tract, gliding along Route 60 where early autumn had stained the fields a dull brown. He felt like a kernel whose outer layers were being teased free. There were so many peeling leaves—Chester, his job, Sarah, Sarah's eyes. Last week at a traffic light close to home he'd caught a glimpse of her studying him. Her hair had nearly hidden her face, but he had recognized the familiar expression. Her eyes probed his brow, the curve of his nose, the pause of his lips. She was looking for a passage back to the generous love they'd once shared. He'd first seen that look six months before and then he had smiled. Later he had realized that if she needed a way back then she must be lost, and he felt a mountain had risen out of the earth between them. He grew anxious and fretful, but then he saw hope: at least she was searching. Her search reassured him and whenever he saw that questioning gaze he waited patiently for her eyes to soften into pools of warm discovery. But last week while they had waited for the light to change her sorrowful eyes had wavered, and she answered him with a dishonest fluttering of her lashes. He accepted her lie with a fraudulent smile of his own, and turned his face back to the traffic light.

About a mile from Kelly's estate the asphalt road became stubbled macadam. A frayed cuff of yellow grass grew beside the curb and this was bordered by a woods of sweet gum, pin oak and maple. Each side of Kelly's gravel driveway was flanked by a row of cedars, and this silent, shaggy retinue ushered Max towards the house.

Max rang the bell three times, then knocked on the heavy door. He stepped back and looked around, but no one was peeking around a window curtain. He banged again, then finally accepted that there would be no reply. He could call on the phone, he could return later, he could pin a note on the door, but the hollow echoes which had answered his knocks had only made him more certain of Kelly's response. He felt sad, he squirmed with an uneasy sense of release, and then he noticed the unfinished foundations. He had no reason to hurry anywhere now and he wandered over to examine them. The trenches lay crumbling, an aborted mess of chunks and clots of concrete. Beyond the foundation he spied another casualty, a wheelbarrow sprayed pink and toppled over. From a different section of the footings rose a jutting that resembled an open hand he'd seen in an art book of Sarah's. Well, this wouldn't be his problem for long.

He returned to the mansion, this time walking around the back side which overlooked the river. From its bluff the view encompassed the whole of the south bank of the James from Surrey on the west down past the hazy clusters of the Idle Fleet, an armada of decommissioned warships anchored midway across the river near Jamestown. It had been a while since he'd seen such a grand horizon, and he paused to take in the wide river, the fuzzy line of trees topping the opposite shore, and the large expanse of milky sky. Then he looked down the bluff. At the end of a small pier he saw Kelly fishing.

One more chance. His heart raced as he hurried down the steps to the pier. He kept his eyes on the painter, but the old man never turned away from his fishing line, and even when Max was finally standing beside him, the old man refused to acknowledge him. Max waited until he felt too uncomfortable to wait any longer. He cleared his throat and said, "Anything biting?"

Kelly wrinkled his nose. "Nothing worth saving."

Max nodded, then walked over to the easel set up near the fishing gear. On the easel was a painting, an abstract of swirling color and form. It meant nothing to Max. He said, "I like the picture."

Kelly finally looked at Max. "You didn't come here to discuss my art or the vagaries of fishing."

"Okay," Max reddened and plunged in, "We both know I'm here to talk about the studio, and I understand, I really do, why you feel that what this Blumkey fellow did was wrong. But I'm not sure you understand how important building this studio is. For a lot of people."

"Including you."

"Like you said, I'm not here for the fishing. Let's face it—you admit you gave him that power, so you know the contract is legal. Maybe I shouldn't be telling you, but they're already studying the papers in the legal contingency department."

"Ahh." Kelly reeled in then cast out again. Finally he said, "Let me give you some advice. If you want to threaten an artist and really frighten him effectively, forget about money. Promise you'll destroy his work or have his name consigned to oblivion. Threaten to invoke the wrath of all that succors his inspiration. In other words, I don't give a fuck about your lawsuit. There will be no studio."

"And there's no chance I can change your mind?" Max tried one last time, but he sensed utter defeat and his sunken face showed it.

"No, but why does all this matter so much to you? What's the worst that can happen?"

"Not much. I'll probably just lose my job and my wife will leave me."

"Yes, life is so tenuous. Just so much vanity and wind. What a lesson this could be for you."

"That's quite—"

Suddenly Kelly's line bent. "Now I've got one," he hissed. He braced himself against the pier's railing, but the fish wasn't much of a fighter, and he relaxed, reeling it in easily. The few times he let the fish run, Max guessed the fisherman was simply prolonging his own pleasure. He watched, impressed by the old man's strength and grace, and when the bent rod straightened, both men stepped up to the railing and looked over the edge. Max was ready to ask what kind of fish he was expecting, when Kelly lifted up his prize, a foot and half long perch. "It's a nice one, yes?" Kelly said as he grasped the fish near its mouth and started twisting his hook free. Amazed, Max watched the fish. It had been years since he'd seen one that wasn't lined up on display beside its buddies on a bed of grocery store ice. He'd forgotten how the living scales glisten in the sun.

He was still watching the fish when Kelly jumped back shouting. The painter hopped and whirled, his hands clutching the perch's mouth. They danced an uncorked jitterbug gone crazy. One wild foot lashed out, sideswiping the open tackle box into a leg of the easel, and a sudden flurry of paint tubes and brushes, hooks, sinkers and lures tumbled onto the pier. A can of wet grass and chopped worms landed on the artist's pallet. Then Max noticed the sprinkle of blood on Kelly's sleeve.

Kelly turned his back to Max and huffed over his shoulder, "The goddam hook's stuck in my thumb." He yanked the fish repeatedly, grunting with each tug, and at last he pulled the perch free. The fish slipped onto the planks, flopped across the tipped over painting, then tumbled into the water.

But in freeing the perch Kelly had sunk the hook deeper into his thumb, and the pain had pushed him to his knees. His good hand cradled its injured twin. Max just watched, still dazed. Kelly's breathing eventually became more even and he muttered at Max, "There should be some wire cutters near the toolbox."

Max found them, but before he gave them to Kelly, he asked, "Is it in past the backhook?"

"Of course it is."

"Then you know the only way to get it out is to push it through. If you pull back you'll just mangle your thumb into hamburger." Kelly didn't move. His cheeks puffed, flabby and pale, and Max asked, "Is that the hand that you paint with?"

Kelly nodded.

Without thinking, Max said, "We both know you can't do it yourself."

Kelly remained hunched over. Max waited patiently, then he raised his eyes to the water. Rogue thoughts unsheathed their daggers—a handle twisting Chester, a flutter eyed Sarah—but Max slipped free of them. He could not coerce the arrogant, old man. He could never make himself that kind of judge. He stared at the gray haze of warships in the distance, and tried to think of nothing. A few seconds later, a tense, reluctant hand tested his palm.

Max dabbed the thumb with his shirt. The finger was swollen and red and smeared with two kinds of blood. He touched the lure and Kelly stiffened. Max said, "Now just hold as still as you can," and without waiting for an answer he grabbed the hook and pushed. Kelly unleashed a howl, tried as hard as he could to snap his hand free, but Max held firmly, he kept pushing, and the back hook followed the point through the skin. Max snipped off the hook and drew the remaining smooth wire back through the thumb. Kelly tugged his hand free, then gingerly wrapped it in a rag and held it to his chest.

Max leaned against the railing. His cheeks were flushed. He wondered if he'd acted like a hero or a coward.

"—Sweet Jesus." Kelly was bent over his painting. It was covered with a wild gyration of fish prints, and a corner swirl of orange and blue was crusted with slime.

More curious than sympathetic, Max asked, "Had you been working on it long?"

"It's never the time." The old man's voice was soft but squeaky. He lifted the painting with his good hand and placed it back upon the easel. For a long time he stared at it with sad eyes, then he suddenly lowered his face to the painting, stepped back, stepped forward, then stepped back again. He rubbed his chin, "Well, why not?"

"Why not what?"

But Kelly was talking to himself. "I can hear the critics now, 'An entirely new concept, one that's radical but bold; natural, and yet transcending the natural. A stunning homage to whimsy.'"

"A what?"

Kelly gestured at the painting. "This painting, young man. You may have just witnessed a moment comparable to Michelangelo ascending the scaffolding or Velázquez arranging his dwarfs."

Max looked at the muck-covered canvas once again. The smell could only get worse. "Are you serious?"

"But of course. And as a token of my appreciation, I'd like to give you this seminal masterpiece."

"Well that's awfully kind of you, but since we're talking about appreciation, what I'd really like is to get back to work on the studio."

Kelly's eyes were glazed, and his voice lifted into delirium. "Forget the studio. Don't you see? There will never be a need for any studios again. We will need piers. We will need docks and bridges. Take this picture and speak to your boss about pilings. Learn everything you can about tides and the sand." He whipped around and walked briskly up the pier. Kelly's bizarre inspiration must have released him from the pain.

"But...."

Kelly turned and Max saw the barest glint of sanity in his eyes. "But if, in some strange turn of events you find yourself so desperate for money that you'd consider parting with 'Fish Corruption, #1', you should contact Blumkey. It should fetch at least eleven or twelve. Do you have his number?"

"Twelve hundred dollars? For this?"

Kelly scowled. "The last time I sold anything for twelve hundred dollars was 1962. Now gather up a few of those loose things and bring them up to the house for me."

Kelly climbed the hill towards the house. Max lifted the canvas and called out to him, "You better call a doctor. You might need stitches or a tetanus shot or something." He looked at the painting, shrugged his shoulders, then replaced it on the easel. He leaned against the railing once more. A glimmer of sunlight rolled a golden swath across the dappled surface of the water. Near the opposite shore, a flock of Canada geese flew just above the woods. Were they flying south already or was their nest close by? Maybe they never flew south at all. He wondered if the fish would live. The geese circled down into the shadows of the cliff and Max carried home his souvenir, the first painting from the fishhook school of art.

REGISTRATION

The rows were packed and the people, silent, strangers to each other, were pressed together. In the middle of a middle row, Alex was unusually sad. So far, being dead was a drag. It was a throbbing ache from sitting too long on a bench with no back. It was pinching regulation shoes and oversized pants that kept slipping down. It was patrols of angels—angels hah, that's a laugh—cracking jokes and watching the clock while making sure all the dead waited peacefully. And this was just registration.

He sat in the largest room he had ever entered, alive or dead. There were no visible walls or ceiling, but he knew he was inside something, a structure that seemed to be modeled after the Astrodome but was spongy and painted a gauzy, snow cloud gray. Along with him were hundreds of thousands of people, perhaps even millions, who remained unassigned. All these people. He had looked around, had nothing else to do but look around, while he waited. Although he had once been a soldier, he had never seen so many kinds of dead people, dead so many kinds of ways. There were umbilical cords that had never stopped bleeding, thighs blueberry blue and ripened by the plague. Emerging from the jungles were pouting gashes of clawed bellies, from Japan an eerie glow of bones burnt and fused. Tribes of starving eyes trickled down his row in succession. The swell of the dead grew tighter.

And then there were those damn angels, nearly identical in appearance, all menacingly bald and dressed in stiff white suits and rainbow sashes and sporting, of course, standard issue gossamer wings with stripes designating rank. The angel patrols wouldn't—or couldn't—enlighten the dead. The answer to any inquiry was the same: "This is just registration. No one has been forgotten. Remain in your seat."

After awhile, the number of questions dwindled.

What particularly oppressed Alex just then was the implication he drew from the sheer numbers of dead who waited and must be as miserable as he was. For surely among all these dead, at least one had reason to be hopeful about the future, at least one must have lived the Right Way, and yet it seemed they had all been sitting there forever, anxious, unassigned and suffering.

It was difficult to feel optimistic.

The man on his left was heavy in a settled sort of way. His face was perpetually morose, with sunken, half-closed eyes, a prominent hooked nose, and a fringe of oiled black and gray hair plastered in a crescent around his scalp. He wore a crumpled, navy pinstripe suit without a tie, and showed no visible cause of death.

"Not what I expected," said Alex.

The man looked straight ahead.

"Been here long?"

The man slowly twisted his head towards Alex, screwed up his eyes, and gave the barest possible nod before turning away.

Everyone on the bench scooted a few inches to the right. Everyone on the opposite bench shifted a few inches to the left.

Alex decided to try one last time. "Heart attack for me. In the elevator on my way to see Vicki. Didn't even make it past the sixth floor. She was a sort of friend of mine. I guess the excitement was too much." He touched his chest. "How about you?"

Alex watched the man take a long, deep breath, watched his face barely tighten, his jaw slightly clench, then relax. The man said nothing, he kept his eyes straight.

Alex turned to the man on the other side of him. He was a short, dirty Nicaraguan peasant with a jagged crater excavated from the back of his skull. Perhaps a .45, at least a .38, Alex decided. "Do you speak English, Amigo?"

"No," said the peasant. "Do you speak Spanish?" Alex shook his head. "That's too bad," the peasant said.

"You speak English pretty good for a man who doesn't speak English."

"You speak Spanish pretty good for a man who doesn't speak Spanish."

They looked at each other. The peasant shrugged.

"This guy," Alex twisted his shoulders to indicate the man in the navy suit, "don't speak at all."

The peasant grimaced and waved his arms across his face. "Fuck him. Who cares? Fuck you, too."

"Hey, watch your mouth, José, I'm a veteran. And don't let this fool you." He patted his paunch. "I ain't afraid to give it out if I have to."

The peasant turned away from Alex, and said to no one in particular, "How can you know what to do? If I give Caesar's hideout to the government, then the government kills him, and his brother kills me. If I don't tell the government, then they kill me. What can you do?"

"Yeah, that's a tough one." Alex puzzled over the dilemma. "I think I'd tell the government and take my chances with the brother. So who got you?"

"My wife."

"Your wife?"

"She found me with her sister, a seventeen year-old with such marangoes...it should be a sin a girl could look so good."

Alex looked at the hole in the man's head and said, "Tough break."

Everyone on the bench scooted a few inches to the right. Everyone on the opposite bench shifted a few inches to the left.

A long time passed and nothing happened. Alex's memories of his past life continued to fade. He seldom thought of Sylvia or their children. Dresden and Korea seemed like dreams. The last traces of ink stains from working the newspaper presses, stains so deep not even the undertaker could remove them, had completely disappeared. It was as if those sixty years had happened to someone else, someone he had once known or read about, and now only a tiny residue of himself remained in the stretched-out empty hand of death.

Then, without warning, the snobbish old man who wouldn't talk said to Alex, "It's time. They're ready for you now." The man swiftly rose, straightened his collar, and proceeded down the row.

The bald angels laughed, prodded one another with their wings, but none interfered. Dumbfounded, Alex stared as the rotund figure with the dignified gait receded into the distance, until finally the message hit home. He jumped off the bench, hollered "Yippie," and swinging his arms in a victory cheer, began to waddle after the man as fast as he could. He passed along rows that stretched as far as he could see, rows crowded with the fidgeting disgruntled company waiting for judgment.

They walked for a long time and as they walked Alex's excitement faded. At first, he had felt smug because he had been chosen while the multitude remained in their seats, but when he considered that he was approaching that final destination (though he had no notion of how much further they would travel), he became afraid and grew angry at the man in the business suit. He was certain the man knew more than he'd revealed.

"You a candy-striper or something, giving guided tours here, or what? You really work for these clowns?"

"Don't we all? Please," said the man, "Don't make this any more difficult for me than it already is. I understand your stress, but believe me, your fate could hardly be worse than my own."

Alex stopped. "I knew it. You knew all along where I was going. Tell me, you filthy bastard. Tell me now."

He grabbed the man by his shirt and raised the sallow face up to his own. "Tell me," he threatened between his teeth. "Tell me or I'll—"

"—Kill me?" He laughed, his thin lips pressed into a mocking grin.

Alex relaxed his grip slightly. "Okay, so maybe I can only rough you up a bit."

"No, no, no, that won't do. That won't do at all. Now, kindly set me free. We really must continue. You don't want to keep them waiting." He spoke rapidly, with the assurance of one who knows.

Frightened, Alex yanked the man closer. He bobbed a frantic meaty fist before the cold eyes. "If I was going to hell, I wouldn't mind keeping them waiting. I wouldn't mind waiting a little longer for that fire and those devils with their pitchforks aiming for my ass."

"You're not going to hell. It doesn't work that way anymore. Now release me this minute so we can continue."

"I'm not going to hell."

"No. You're not going to hell. I told you. It's not like that." With cautious eyes fastened on Alex, the man withdrew from his grasp as gingerly as if he were disengaging his suit from a thorn bush. "Be reasonable," he murmured in a soothing tone, "I've already told you a great deal, much more than usual and certainly more than is permitted. So be a good fellow, Alex, calm yourself with a deep breath or two—that's it—in and out, in and out. Now let's continue on our way."

Alex exhaled deeply, regarded his sore feet, and nodded.

Satisfied, the businessman turned and as if to make up for lost time, he hastened down the row. "And please, please, please, no more questions," he called back over his shoulder. "I warn you, I shall refuse to answer."

At first resigned, Alex trudged along the unending path, but gradually his spirits improved—after all, it was true he wasn't sitting and the old man had promised he wasn't going to hell. Death was looking better all the time. Perhaps they'd allow him to say a few words about himself. He searched through his memories for an appropriate and revealing incident, but everything appeared so shrouded and vague that he decided to be spontaneous. He would speak simply and honestly from his heart when the big moment arrived.

The benches ceased and Alex and the businessman stopped before a mahogany desk, ornately carved and twice the size of a cathedral organ. Two angels were typing at incredibly rapid speeds on their computer keyboards. They were unlike the other angels he had seen. One was fat, with bushy eyebrows and a greasy, unshaven face. If angels wore lapels instead of wings, his would have been stained with mustard. The second was tall, thin and phthisic, and his fine platinum hair was coiled in a braid that rested on the back of his neck. His watery eyes were so gray they were nearly colorless.

The fat angel looked up from his work. Reams of computer printouts leaning like snow drifts tumbled off his side of the desk. He laughed heartily when he saw the businessman. "Well, Big D., welcome. Welcome. I hope we enjoyed a nice walk?"

The businessman swallowed and asked, "Can we just get on with it?"

Alex stepped forward, "I'd like to say a few words, if I may."

"It's really not necessary," the thin angel dismissed him with a wave of a bony hand. "Your file's quite complete. We may be slow, but we do know everything."

"But—"

"Please," he continued, "You've seen the line."

The businessman spoke up. "I'd like this one, if you've no objection. It's been awhile since you've given me one, and you both know it is my right. He's been completely insufferable. You saw how he grabbed and threatened me. I could do wonders with him. Surely you can see that."

"Stop calling me Shirley," chuckled the fat angel, picking his teeth with a corner of the printout.

The second angel said, "I'd like to help you, Danny boy, but there's pressure on us, too. We're doing the Russians this month. All the Russians. Rumor has it He's throwing some kind of festival. And you know what it's like when we do the Russians."

"Especially when there are no good wars going on," said the first angel after wiping his blubbery lips with his sleeve. "We all have to sacrifice when He goes on these Russian kicks."

Alex cleared his throat. "Um, pardon me, but could somebody explain exactly what is going on?"

Danny asked, "May I?"

"It's the least we can do for you," said the thin one.

"And the most that we will," added the other.

Danny twisted the ends of his lips into his thin smile and narrowed his eyes upon Alex. He slowly raised his hands before his face, spreading the fingers wide so that each rested lightly on the tip of its counterpart. "Ah Alex, what image shall I use for you? Nothing too rich or complex, no." He closed his eyes and appeared deep in thought.

"Let's go, Big D. You know we're operating under a deadline here," the first angel said impatiently, drumming his round fingers against a stack of papers.

"Then I suppose the usual explanation will have to suffice," Danny sighed, disappointment filling his voice. "Imagine you're an actor, Alex, and this, all of this," he opened his eyes and waved his arms in a sweeping gesture, "is a tremendous movie studio. These angels are employed in Central Casting, and their job is to assign you a role—not a movie role—but rather your particular role in the next life." He turned to the angels, "It's rather clear so far, isn't it?"

"Like where I'll be born, who my parents will be, that sort of thing?"

"That and a little more. You see, these roles are a bit more precise than what you have in mind. You're going to become a specific fictional character, a Russian one, it would seem. Apparently, you will speak the tongue of the Tsars in your next life. Unless, of course, you appear in translation."

"I'm like an actor in a play?"

"No, not at all. You won't be going home for cigars and brandy after a two hour performance. From what I've been told it all seems quite real, at least in the better texts."

"I believe that's sufficient," said the thin angel. "We really must continue. I believe we'd discussed him for Vronsky."

"No, no," the fat angel disagreed, "Vronsky's much too smooth for this guy, much too sophisticated. And with that face, forget it. Make him a philandering soldier from the barracks. We must need plenty of them."

"Look, I agree he's not the best Vronsky, and I know that *Anna Karenina* is a personal favorite, but as you so accurately pointed out, we have a deadline." The thin angel typed a few letters on the keyboard and nodded at the monitor screen. "Just look at his underlying grid: military service, the sex and death connection, and look—for Christ's sake—he even has the right first name. Think how much easier the paperwork will be."

The angels continued to argue but Alex was too stunned to listen. None of it made any sense. He turned to the businessman, "They're really going to stick me in a Russian novel?" Danny nodded then smirked while the angels quarreled over Alex becoming this character named Vronsky. Stomach acid surged into Alex's throat. Who could've imagined death was such a thing, to be tossed into a book by some angel? And a commie book at that. What had he done that was so horrible he deserved to come back as a Russian, as one of the enemy? He wondered if there were any way to appeal the decision.

Abruptly, the angels stopped quarreling and Danny stiffened. A small, wiry, olive skinned man approached and waved to the angels, "Hey guys."

The angels saluted crisply.

"Oh, cut it out. How many times do I have to tell you, save it for the Old Man, okay?" He smiled at Alex. It was the kindest smile Alex had ever seen. There was more love and compassion in his face than Alex had experienced in an entire lifetime. The man leaned over to inspect the thin angel's computer monitor, and his expression changed, his brow wrinkled in confusion. "Vronsky? This guy?"

"It wasn't my idea," the fat angel answered quickly.

The other protested, "You know how we're working under a terrible strain. The pressure to fill all these roles...I mean look at this list. Just look at it." His fragile, almost translucent, arms lifted the top hundred pages of the huge printout, and hundreds more cascaded onto the floor.

"I know, I know," he answered sympathetically. "I've talked to Him about this before, but you know how He can be: He is Who He is. You guys do what you think is best."

The small man started to leave when Alex stepped forward. "Excuse me, sir, but these angels here made a mistake. They're putting me into a Russian book, and that can't be right. I know I wasn't a saint or anything, at least I think I wasn't, but I couldn't have done anything so bad that I should be turned into a communist."

The fat angel snickered, "You see what I'm saying. But if you want a moron for Vronsky, I agree. You've found your man."

The wiry man frowned and waved a smooth finger at the angel, "Remember, there's a reason why you're only in 'Roles and Registration'." Then he rested his gentle hands on Alex's shoulders. "Just relax. I know where you're coming from—I've been there myself. Everything will be fine. You don't know very much about literature, do you Alex?"

"Ahh, no sir. O-only what I read."

"Yes, I understand. Don't worry, the Russians can be quite enjoyable.

Believe me, there are worse punishments, much worse. One Nazi—I won't name names, you understand, but believe me, his is one you'd recognize—is on his second go round of Barthelme."

The fat angel jabbed his elbow into the skinny one and laughed, "The dumb kraut can't even finish a sentence anymore."

The small, gentle man ignored this and continued, "I'd say, just judging from your file, I'd say you were no worse than average. But let me give you one bit of advice for this next time." He pulled Alex one step nearer.

"Certainly," said Alex, somewhat relieved by this assurance, and pledging to live better so that the next time he could return as an American. "I'm sure anything you tell me will get me off to a good start."

"Boots," he said, his kind eyes shining for Alex. "Good boots. Always keep a pair around. Never, absolutely never, get caught in Russia with a pair of lousy boots. Believe me, you'll wish you were dead." He turned to the angels. "Well, I do have my appearances to make—"

The thin angel asked, "Can we pencil you in for that small part in *The Brothers Karamozov*? I noticed the last time you seemed to enjoy it so much."

"I did enjoy that. Yes, that sounds quite nice," he replied and then patting Alex on the shoulder he said, "Keep the faith, man." He removed his hand and walked away, his white robe trailing behind him. The two angels typed until he was no longer in view.

"He is who I think he is, isn't he?" Alex asked the angels.

The fat one said, "He's considered One Major Dude in these parts, if that's what you mean. Couldn't you tell from the way old boneface here bellied up to him." He pursed his lips, "'Can we pencil you in for that small part in *The Brothers Karamozov*?...I noticed the last time you seemed to enjoy it so much.' Give me a break."

"You think you're so smart," the pale angel said heatedly, his gray eyes tearing. "But one day, one day he's not going to forgive and forget and you'll find yourself working for the famous Italian here." He pointed at Danny.

"Yes," Danny said, "Now there's a prospect I could relish, but can we please get on with this?"

"Why?" Alex asked.

"Because we've wasted enough time already," Danny answered impatiently.

"No, I mean, Why?"

"He means the big Why, Danny," the thin angel said.

A buzzer rang above the fat angel's desk, and he grinned at Danny. "Sorry, no assignments for the next ten minutes. Union rules." He opened a drawer in his desk, and removed a plump cigar which he unwrapped and lit. After taking a couple of puffs he said, "You see, Alex, things were becoming rather boring here. I mean, let's face it, not much was changing in heaven or hell. Same old paradise, same old fires of perdition. It was dull. In the meantime, over where you were, people were writing like never before, turning out all kinds of fiction. So," he inhaled, then released a cloud of gray smoke, "So, one day the Big Man calls a meeting, sets up a Joint Commission for the Sequential Transition of Afterlife Alteration and this is what we end up with. You know, technology here is only a snap of The Fingers. Sure, it seems dishonest, but who's going to sue? And with the notable exception of us poor schmucks stuck here on the front lines," he pointed to the other angel and himself with the cigar, "the system runs like a dream. The Old Man is amused, and even his old, hard-line cronies over in Justice are happy."

Danny interrupted, "Please, he hasn't the slightest idea what you're talking about. It would be easier to initiate a horse into the mysteries of quantum mechanics than to teach this philistine the most primitive concept. No wonder you can't meet a deadline, you never do any work. Union rules, my ass. Besides, the sooner we finish with him, the sooner you can do something worthwhile. Like my Comedy. It's been nearly a century. I deserve better, you know. Everyone says I deserve better."

Alex looked at Danny with astonishment and then turned to the angels. "Shit," he said, "If this guy is a comedian you jokers have more problems than I thought."

"Please let me have him. Please," begged Danny. "I promise not to quibble over which circle, either. Any one you choose is fine with me."

"Don't worry, Dan," the fat angel said, his face surrounded by a halo of cigar smoke. "No one's forgotten you. I've stashed away a Nicaraguan peasant who was simply made for your fifth canto. He's an ace, a shooting star. A little plastic surgery to the skull and you'll swear he was born for the part."

The buzzer sounded once more.

The thin angel turned to the fat one, his finger poised above a button on his console. "Vronsky, Okay? Next time, it's your choice. I promise."

The fat angel shrugged his shoulders, then nodded.

He rubbed his eyes, missing what the countess beside him on the couch was saying, and when he looked up old Princess Scherbatsky was smiling at him with her head inclined towards a tall, strongly built man who appeared ill at ease. "'Let me introduce you' said the princess, nodding at the man, 'Constantine Dmitrich Levin, Count Alexis Kirilovich Vronsky.'

"Vronsky got up and with a friendly look into Levin's eyes shook his hand.

"'I think I was to have dined with you earlier this winter,' Vronsky said with his simple, open smile, 'but you went off to the country unexpectedly....'"

SECOND STRIKES

The first time he saw the bugs, Matthew blamed the rain. A harrowing spring torrent had soaked the earth all morning, and when at last the cold shower had passed and the sky had hinted brightness, the insects appeared. They were shiny and black and no longer than a child's fingernail. Matthew guessed they had ascended along the pipe that rose from his basement and fed the radiator in the living room. From the radiator the insects fanned out in all directions. While his wife ran to get the bug spray from the cabinet high above the kitchen sink, Matthew surveyed the room. Some insects lined a narrow path to the fireplace. Others had blazed a trail behind the sofa. Many of these had died though Matthew wasn't sure what had killed them. A few survivors crawled in ragged circles.

When Vera returned she carried the vacuum cleaner in one hand and the can of Black Flag in the other. Matthew plugged in the vacuum and with the extension hose he sucked up the bugs, first the living ones, then the dead along the trail leading back to the radiator. Where the pipe pierced the living room floor there were more than one hundred of them, their gray translucent wings folded back, all dead. When he had finished vacuuming Vera sprayed the pipe and surrounding carpet with Black Flag. A filmy cloud rose searing their eyes and throats, and swept them out coughing to the front steps.

"I'm glad the girls weren't home." Matthew said as he sipped a diet Pepsi to remove the taste of the Black Flag. "They'd have a fit if they saw those bugs."

"What do you think they are? Termites?" Vera rubbed her eyes.

"I don't know. On TV, termites are small and a chalky white color. But at least they're gone now. You want some?" He raised the can to her.

She shook her head. "Well, they may be gone now, but they could come back. Don't you think we should call the exterminator?"

"Let's wait and see. Maybe it was a fluke kind of thing."

"Maybe," she sighed, tucking a few strands of thin brown hair behind her ear. When they were first married, Vera had worn her hair long, but she had clipped it short when the children in her special ed class wouldn't stop pulling on it. Occasionally, she'd forget it was short, and Matthew would smile to himself when he caught her, flattening her palms along her scalp as if to gather the absent tresses into a ponytail.

A few weeks passed and Matthew did not see any more bugs, but then another heavy storm drenched the neighborhood and that afternoon the insects appeared along the base of the radiator. This time, Shelly and Clarissa found them while Vera was cooking dinner.

"What did you do about them?" he asked Vera.

"*I* vacuumed and sprayed like before. Can't you smell it? Then *I* called the exterminator. He's coming Wednesday but *I* have to work. Can you come home early to let him in?"

"If you can't, I guess I'll have to."

"We have to do something."

Matthew ran his hand across Shelley's head and nodded.

The exterminator who came on Wednesday was a young Black man. He wore a neatly pressed maroon uniform with a patch on the chest that had "Davis" sewn in a clean flowing script. He was a few inches shorter than Matthew, but while Matthew was built loose and soft, Davis' arms were hard, his body wiry, and he was full of energy. Davis narrowed his brown eyes and listened intently as Matthew described the appearance of the bugs and where he had found them. When Matthew finished talking, the exterminator paced rapidly back and forth across the living room. He pulled the sofa away from the radiator and kneeled down, sticking his nose against the painted metal pipes. "Yes, yes," he kept repeating to himself. Matthew wanted to know "yes what?" but he waited. He would find out soon enough. What was he going to do if he had termites in his house? He had always feared something like this would happen. Davis rooted around, looking at other radiators on the first floor. Then he ran down the steps and began checking the joists in the basement ceiling, stabbing them with a pocket knife. When he finished with the joists, he inspected the ground level windows, which allowed a few rays of sunlight into the cellar. Matthew heard a sick crunch as the knife punched through a sill. The young man seemed pleased with the results. For close to an hour Matthew had been following him around like a puppy, and at last he could contain himself no more. "Well, is it termites?"

"Yes, indeed, it's termites." Matthew's heart froze. His house had just received a death sentence. He could picture Vera tossing all their possessions

97

into boxes, shooing out the girls in a whirling hurry just as the roof caved in. A hurricane of bugs was poised to strike at any second. He swallowed hard.

"How bad is it? Is there anything you can do?"

Davis heard the fear in his voice and looked away from the ceiling. He studied Matthew curiously. "Don't sweat it man, you're OK. Check this out." He poked the ceiling joist again. The wood responded with a hard, sturdy thud. "That's a good sound there. No structure damage. You just got a rotten windowsill. The rest of your house is in fine shape. This is what I'd call a mild termite problem." Matthew instantly liked him and Davis smiled when he saw Matthew's relief. Davis said, "Let's go outside and see if we can find where they're coming from."

The exterminator bounded up the basement steps two at a time, then rushed through the door and into the yard. He stopped next to the oak which towered outside the living room window.

"Yes, yes, yes," he said, nodding his head vigorously. "You got to get rid of this sucker. It's rotten, man. You knew that, didn't you? It's deader than shit. This tree's been dead a long time. You got to chop this sucker down." Davis launched into a detailed explanation of his two-pronged attack to save Matthew's home. The first part was the cure, ridding the house of termites. He showed Matthew how he would drill cores three feet deep into the ground surrounding the house. By filling the cores with an insecticide, he would create a barrier to keep the termites away. The second prong was prevention, and that meant getting rid of the nest the termites had built. The only way to do that was to chop down the tree. "Some termites get killed by the barrier, the rest lose their home. They decide staying around here is too much trouble, so they go somewhere else. I get a new house to fix and you get a termite free home. How's that sound?" He gave Matthew a big smile.

"Do we really have to cut down the tree? Won't that barrier be good enough?"

Davis frowned and rubbed his toe into the ground like he was crushing a cigarette. "Well, the barrier will work for a while, but sooner or later they'll come back. Insecticides don't last forever, you know. And besides, you still got a rotten tree."

"Yeah," Matthew sighed, his voice far away.

"Well, you think about it. I've got two more houses to check before lunch and I'm already starving. I'll be back next week to put the barrier in. You do what you want about the tree."

When Davis had driven away, Matthew went back to the oak and pushed on it as hard as he could. It seemed pretty solid. The tree was over forty feet tall. Matthew guessed it was a sapling when the house was first built. Perhaps the original owner, now dead for many years, had planted the tree to commemorate a birth or a child's wedding. Matthew felt the tree was as much a part of this house as the bedrooms and the back porch.

He thought back to the night five years ago when lightning had struck the tree. He had been asleep, but the noise had awakened Vera and terrified the girls. They came screaming into his bedroom and scrambled under the covers, clinging to Matthew and Vera. He treasured that memory because it was the last time since they were babies that all of them had slept together. He remembered the crowded warmth of the bed, the snug happiness of having his whole family under the blankets. Outside the thunder raged and the rain whipped against the windows. He could not recall another storm quite like that one.

The next morning after the storm had ended, he surveyed the damage. A gaping chasm ran down the middle of the tree. The bark was stripped and the inner core cracked and jagged. He climbed a ladder and stuck his face inside the dark cavity. His nostrils flared at the sour smell. When he withdrew his head he discovered his neighbor Buddy Milton standing at the foot of the ladder squinting up at him. An orange baseball cap was pushed down over his head. Buddy said, "That was one dilly of a lightning bolt."

"Yeah, it woke up my girls and gave them a quite a scare."

"Just the girls? You mean you slept through that racket?" Matthew nodded as he finished descending the ladder and Buddy shook his head. "I can't believe it. That lightning nearly blew up the tree, woke up half the neighbors, and you slept right through it? You're damn lucky, fella."

"'Cause I slept through the lightning?"

"No, no." Buddy grimaced waving his hands at the bough. "If that tree hadn't been there, that lightning probably would've hit your house." Matthew hadn't considered that. "On the other hand, the tree looks shot to shit. Let me take a look."

Buddy started up the ladder before Matthew could reply and poked his head into the burnt out hole in the trunk. He pulled a knife out of his jeans and chiseled off a sliver of wood. He held that up and inspected it carefully. His squinting face reminded Matthew of a wrinkled prune. Buddy looked down from the ladder as if he were a judge passing sentence. "You better call a tree surgeon. This oak is on life support."

Matthew shrugged his shoulders and pushed his hands deeper into his pockets as he looked away. "I guess so."

A few weeks passed before Matthew got around to calling a tree surgeon. The tree surgeon agreed that the tree should come down but when Matthew pressed him for alternatives, he offered to plaster the gash with a black tarry substance. The surgeon didn't expect it to work, but Matthew chose that approach since it seemed to be the only possible way to save the tree. The following spring, much to Matthew's surprise, the tree had put out leaves, but only on one side. With each passing year the number of branches sprouting leaves had dwindled. The last two springs the tree had sprouted no leaves at all, but Matthew ignored the obvious. Now, staring at the top of the barren tree, he wondered if the termites that invaded his house had been sent as punishment for his neglect. Perhaps he deserved this because he had buried his head in the sand. "Termites and rotten trees," he sighed.

When Vera arrived home from school Matthew told her about Davis' two-pronged attack. "Well, I'm not surprised," she said. "I didn't think the tree would last this long. And the last thing we need is more termites. Maybe you should talk to Buddy? He'll know what to do."

"Yeah, and if he doesn't, he'll tell me anyway. But I'll talk to him if it'll make you happy." Matthew knew Vera was right. Buddy would have a solution for the problem. Buddy had a solution for every problem. Matthew thought it was because he was from the Midwest – Wisconsin or was it Indiana? – Matthew couldn't remember. People who grew up there had great stores of practical knowledge. They seemed to be born knowing how to fix tractors, milk cows and jerry-rig a thing so it would work. Whenever Matthew went to ask Buddy a question, he always found him hammering something onto something else.

When Buddy came over the next day to inspect the tree Matthew told him about the termites. "But I still don't know about cutting the thing down. It's not the money. I just like the tree. It just seems to belong here, like it's a part of the house."

"You're right about one thing. It's gonna be part of your house when it falls right on top of it. It's rotten Matthew. You should have taken it out years ago. I told you that after that big storm. A tree this close to a house is dangerous anyway, but this one's dead. It's got no strength, no resistance. It could fall anytime."

"I don't know, Buddy."

"Look. Me and you can do it together with my chainsaw. It'll take a few hours. Shoot. I've cut down bigger by myself. And you'll get some decent firewood too."

"Those chainsaws make an awful lot of noise. It would scare my girls."

Buddy lifted his gaze to the top of the tree, but Matthew wondered if he wasn't really looking higher, appealing to some heavenly source to help him explain the obvious to his idiot neighbor. Finally, Buddy said, "Well, it's your house and your tree. But one day it's gonna fall. And if it crashes through your roof it's gonna scare those kids a hell of a lot more than my chainsaw. You think about it. I'll be ready when you are."

Davis came the next week and drilled the cores. When the next storm came through, Matthew waited expectantly for the termites to appear, but there were none. After each rain for the rest of that spring Matthew expected to find termites, but none appeared in the house. As spring turned to summer, Matthew relaxed. He also thought less often about the tree, although every week or two while he was doing yard work he would lean against the oak or give it a strong shove. The large tree never budged. It seemed sturdy. Sometimes when he saw Buddy, Matthew would feel a guilty twinge, but he made no plans to cut down the tree.

Each June, after the end of the school year, Vera took the girls for a two week trip to visit her mother in Norfolk. Her father had been in the Navy and after his retirement they had built a home there. When he died her mother, having already uprooted her household at least a half a dozen times, was content to remain where they had last settled. The night before Vera and girls left was always difficult for Matthew. He could already taste the force of their absence and he did not even have the slight consolation of thinking that, say, three days had passed, so only eleven more remained until their return. The countdown to their reunion had not yet even begun and he was miserable.

Vera could see how unhappy he was. "You should keep busy while we're gone. Do things to keep your mind occupied."

"Like what?"

"Well, you could clean out the basement. You've been putting that off for a while. Or, maybe, you and Buddy could cut down that tree."

He laughed. "You know I can't do anything while you're gone."

"Why not? You have too many girls lined up?" she teased. They laughed and he hugged her. "This would be the perfect time to do it." She said as they embraced.

"Do what?" he asked. And when she didn't answer, he said, "I'll think about it."

In the morning, he drove them to the train station and helped them load the baggage onto the racks above their seats. He gave each of the girls a ten dollar bill and remained on the train until the last possible moment. He waited on the platform until the train disappeared around the curve and then, lonely as a forgotten astronaut, he returned to his car. Matthew's tendency was to stray to the morose when he was alone and it descended upon him now. He remembered taking Clarissa to the pediatrician for what he thought was a routine stomachache but turned out to be appendicitis. He had sat sweating, staring at his pale hands during her surgery, wondering if this was the day his life changed. It could have happened. It could still happen any day. A drunk driver could smash into their school bus. Another child could throw acid at her face to steal her lunch money. He had read about that in the paper. It had happened to a girl in a different school last month. Or one of them could be molested or kidnapped. Even his gas bill came with an enclosure, a fuzzy black and white photo of a child above the pleading caption: "DO YOU KNOW ME?"

And Vera. He knew most men would find her plain. The forty pounds she had gained during her pregnancy with Shelly had settled around her waist and hips; but Matthew saw only her eyes, deep blue and beautiful, those eyes full of compassion and patience. She needed that patience to teach those children in school. Or to put up with him. They had a good marriage, and he knew that. But who was invulnerable? Nobody. So Matthew worried a little when her bus was late, or even when she went to the doctor for a routine check-up. Disaster could announce itself that way. It wasn't likely, but it could. Every day it happened just like that to someone, somewhere. Or despite everything he thought he understood, she could fall out of love with him. He might come home one day and find she had packed her bags and left him. He thought of all their friends who never laughed or were divorced.

He knew there was nothing profound or unique about his worries, but that did not ease his nights. His one slight comfort was his suspicion that he was somehow safe, that he had been randomly chosen or passed over. Each sunset seemed to confirm it. Nothing bad had happened yet. He felt like a small forest creature who hears its predator lurking nearby and knows its best chance to survive is to hide in the shadows. Maybe the beast will pass. He remained still, horribly still, afraid to move or act for fear that he would call attention to his good luck. Matthew was wary of his happiness because he knew he had done so little to deserve it; or rather, he knew there were many people, just as deserving, who had suffered great losses.

When Vera and the girls returned from their trip, the tree remained standing beside the house. Vera glanced at the tree, then gave Matthew a meaningful look, but she said nothing. For the rest of the summer, Matthew was busy at work. It was unusually hot and Vera and the girls spent most of their days at the neighborhood pool. When Matthew worked late Vera would bring the children home for an early supper and then they would return to swim some more. When Matthew finally left work he would stop to retrieve them. He would pause, his back against the fence surrounding the pool and wait until they spotted him. What beautiful girls, he thought, watching them bounce and swim. Each day he snapped another mental photograph: hair damp, shiny, and slick upon their scalps; mischievous eyes smiling and red from chlorine; thin legs browned from long days in the sun. When they saw him they would run up and he would gather them close. On evenings when a slight breeze blew, their lips would blush purple and they would shiver wrapped in towels until Vera could rush them into the tub. Those nights filled him with great joy. He could not remember a happier time.

On a Saturday afternoon in late August, Matthew was watching a baseball game on TV. The Phillies and Mets were in a tight division race that year and though he was only a casual fan he thought this game could be exciting. He stretched out on the sofa, sipping on a beer that had lost its chill two innings ago. The Phillies had just turned a double play to end the sixth inning when Clarissa rushed through the door. "Daddy, Daddy, come quick. Shelly fell in a hole."

Matthew wanted to ask what hole but Clarissa was already out the door. They ran to the bottom of the street where the gas company had been working. One of the two large metal plates that covered the work area had been moved aside and he heard Shelly crying. He peered into the crater which looked to be five feet deep. Shelly saw him and howled louder. "I'm coming sweetie." Matthew's heart was pounding. He gripped the side of the plate and lowered himself down, feeling carefully for the bottom and the gas pipe. "I'm coming Shelly, I'm coming." His foot touched the gas main and he carefully tested to see if it would support his weight. Nothing moved. He was sweating well beyond what the heat would provoke. Shelly's eyes were dark and pleading in a way he had never seen them before. She had some small scrapes on her legs, but seemed otherwise fine. She jumped to hug him tightly. He held her close for a moment, trying hard not to think about anything. "Ok, I'm going to lift you up and push you over the top. You can do this, Shelly. You're my big girl. You can do this." He was surprised his voice was so soothing and sure. He lifted her up and grunting, pushed her over the rim. Once she was over, he jumped as hard as he could off the pipe, pushed down on the edge and tugged himself up. He was dirty, sweating wildly, his heart pounding. "Jesus," he muttered. The two girls looked down at him as he sat on the ground catching his breath. He smiled up at them. "Let's go home."

"You saved her Daddy!"

"Yes," he said. "Yes I did."

Matthew put his arms around them while they walked back to the house. What would Vera say? Who had moved that metal plate? On Monday morning Matthew called the tree surgeon and told him to come take down the tree as soon as possible.

THE DUEL

I had downed my nightly Seconal, brushed my teeth and flossed, and was dreaming under a magazine when a furious pounding on the door downstairs aroused me from my slumber. Beside me, my wife Eleanor, despite my repeated nudging, snored the sleep of the forgetful; so, with a groggy yawn and sigh, I slipped into my robe and slippers. The savage knocking began afresh as I cautiously approached the door. Who could be the source of such commotion at this late hour? Probably someone was lost.

But no, it was Razor Roundtree. "Open the door, you bastard," he bellowed. I was delighted and surprised. I hadn't seen him in years, but with Razor, that was hardly unusual. "Good to see you, Ace. Let's have a drink," he cried as he engulfed me in his warmest of hugs. When he finally released me, he marched unerringly straight to the liquor cabinet, (although he had never before been in my house), proceeded to pour himself a large glass of expensive Scotch (the Scotch I sip on those rare special occasions), gulped down the amber liquid, and pulled down another tumbler which he filled for me before topping off his own once more. "Old friends," he said cheerily as he clinked his glass against mine. The pupils in his bright green eyes were wildly dilated, perhaps from the effects of drugs or alcohol, perhaps just naturally. With Razor one guess was as good as another at any given moment. He quaffed down his drink and poured himself a third. Yes, old Razor looked the same as always. He was an imposing figure as he stood over six and a half feet tall with the thick trunk, broad shoulders and strong arms of a wrestler. Except for a large cleft in his chin, his features were solid, regular, and the unkempt curly blonde locks that spilled onto his forehead forever charmed the women. His dress consisted of dirty green pants, an old inverness coat with flapping cape and tight round collar, and a battered deerstalker cap. All in all, he resembled a bear which had escaped from a Sherlock Holmes look-alike contest.

"Where the hell have you been?"

"I was visiting my sweet Belinda," he answered, raising one cunning eyebrow. "She hangs out at this bar that had their annual costume party tonight. I made it to the final round in this Sherlock Holmes disguise," he said proudly as he opened wide his cape.

"So that's who you're supposed to be," I answered dryly. "But I can't imagine Belinda as Watson. What did she wear?"
He roared with laughter, "Oh you know Belinda – very little. And with her, no costume is definitely the best costume of all."

"Of course. And she probably won." I looked into my drink and asked him, "So, what kind of trouble are you into now?"

"We'll get to that later. Nothing too serious. What ho! What's this?" he asked in his faux Holmes accent as my old basset hound, Newton, waddled in to inspect the late night visitor. Razor scratched the dog vigorously behind its ears, which cause Newton to grin and drool upon the living room carpet. "Whoa! You ever bathe this mutt?" Newton does carry his own distinct aroma.

"You've never met Newton? No matter, let's get back to my question. What kind of trouble are you in now?" Razor and trouble were like, well, like Holmes and Watson. Where one was snooping, the other was sure to follow. You could easily figure that an adventure with Razor Roundtree would leave you explaining something farfetched to the law, the mob, the doctor, the priest or some bizarre combination of them all. I remembered the time he had been so drunk he had driven his car through the plate glass front of an all-night convenience store. Needless to say, this was a convenience they had not intended on providing. The police had summoned my father to the station house where he bailed Razor out, then squared things with the judge. And there was the time when, as a runner for a cocaine dealer, Razor found himself in possession of an unusually pure batch of the drug. To correct this oversight, he cut the pure two kilos into four impure ones and kept half for himself. His employer quickly detected what had happened, despite all of Razor's protests to the contrary; and Razor's apartment, his car, and other anticipated hiding places were carefully scrutinized, which is to say vandalized, by quiet men in custom fitted suits and shiny pointed shoes. I was certain Razor's own wardrobe was about to include one final cement bathing suit, designed but for a single wearing; however, much to my surprise and great relief, when no cocaine was found, Razor was set free. He kept the cocaine in a lock box under my mother's azalea bushes for another three months before he sold it. And then there was the time... but you get the idea.

He was truly more my younger brother's friend than mine although we all considered him one of the family. His parents had died when he was young and he had been thrust upon a maiden aunt who had little use for children, less for little boys, and even less for a scamp like Razor. This maiden aunt, our next door neighbor, raised him the best she could, given that she couldn't stand the child. I suppose my parents were more tolerant of his shenanigans because he wasn't their son. God alone knows what they would have done to my brother if their roles had been reversed.

"So what is it this time?" I asked again, when we had settled into our chairs in the living room.

"I need a second and as I don't know anyone else still living in this God forsaken town, I thought of you. You don't mind, do you? It'll only take a little of your time."

"I'm sorry Razor, I must have had more to drink than I thought. What do you mean 'a second?' The only kind of second I know of is in a duel."

"Precisely, Ace," he shouted exuberantly, picking up that accent again. "Oh, sorry, mustn't awaken the misuss. Yes, but you hit it right on the nose. You always were the smart one in the family. I'm fighting a duel in the morning and I need a second."

I nearly spit out my drink. "You're serious?"

"Completely. Tomorrow morning, pistols at twelve paces. Well, will you do it?"

"My God, you are serious." I stopped to think for a moment. "I'm giving a phyiscs test first period tomorrow. I can't miss that."

"No problem, the duel's at dawn. You'll be at school in plenty of time. So, then it's settled. A toast to the duelist and his second!" and he pulled down the Chivas and poured us each another glass.

"Hold on, Razor. Aside from the fact that you might lose, which could have grave consequences for any future plans you may have, isn't this against the law? Wouldn't I be an accomplice or something? I don't think the school board would take it the right way. I don't think that I take it the right way. And who are you dueling with and what about, anyway?"

He leaned forward in his chair. "I thought you'd never ask. Do you remember the year I spent at the Military Institute?"

"I thought you were expelled during the second semester—"

"Just listen. Of course you remember. Well, I don't know if Tom ever told you, but the reason I was expelled had nothing to do with my grades. Not that my grades were so wonderful, but I was expelled after the commandant's wife and I were found in bed together. The woman was a clever bitch. We went from passion to rape in a fraction of a second and her fool of a husband believed every word of it. What a pompous idiot. Of course, he had enough sense not to call the police. They'd have laughed him right out of town. So now he's challenged me to a duel." Razor pursed his lips in imitation of the commandant. "'And so, Mr. Roundtree, this duel is the only recourse that remains for an honorable gentleman who needs to avenge the indignity you've perpetrated upon his pitiful and defenseless wife.' What a crock of shit. But you know the military—no brains, no money—but plenty of honor and bravery," he laughed. "If honor and bravery are one side of the record, the flip side is stupidity."

I could barely control my alarm. "Razor, this guy is not only out of his mind, he's out of his century. I mean, this sounds like something that might have happened a few hundred years ago, but this is the 1980's. Adultery happens all the time now, and people don't fight duels about it. They're either hurt or they're relieved, but they don't shoot anybody. And why is it coming up now, so many years later? You want my advice? Skip town and forget the whole thing."

"Ace," His tone suddenly became serious. "I can't just run away. Not because of my own sense of honor— we both know I have none—but because you're right. This guy is crazy. If I disappear now, what's to keep him from tracking me down and shooting me in the back? The man is serious, very serious. Obviously, he's been obsessed with this affair for years. At least in a duel I have a chance." The gleam in his eye had disappeared, and I knew this was a more earnest Razor than I had ever seen before. I cleared my throat. "Here. Have another drink." And I reached for the bottle and poured one for each of us.

In the living room we drank scotch as we reminisced about the old days, our deceased parents, our long lost friends until eventually I passed out in my chair. Sometime later, a steady tugging on my shoulder aroused me. "Come on Ace. It's time." I spent a hazy moment in the darkness trying to discern who he was; for his usually cherubic face was quite pale and stern, was ghostly unfamiliar as he loomed above me. Like devils that refuse to leave our dreams, I found upon awakening I had acquired two other unwanted companions: the dull, throbbing headache and queasy stomach that follow a night of foolish indulgence. I dressed quietly in the closet, brushed and flossed my teeth again, and lightly kissed my still snoring wife goodbye. These rituals of the morning seemed to frighten those demons, seemed to push them back towards their homes in the night. And so my head was almost clear when we descended the front steps of the house. With little ceremony, I opened the passenger door of my Malibu for Razor and we drove in silence to the park.

We hiked along a trail that parallels McCormick Creek on its course to the river. Even in the pre-dawn light I could distinguish the bright green on the fingertip sprouts of evergreens and in the flashing leaves of oaks and maples. Pink cherry blossoms and petals of white dogwood lined the path as I followed Razor to his fate. "I never thought I'd be the one you'd come to for something like this," I confessed.

"Well, that's the wonderful thing about life, isn't it?"

"But isn't there another way to resolve this?" I was behind him on the trail. He stopped and turned to face me. His cold eyes burned through the crisp chill of the morning, and that look was sufficient response. He said nothing.

As we silently continued our trek, I conjured up the many volleys of imaginary bullets I had fired in my physics classes. Invariably, I would miss the mark in these attempts to teach my indifferent students about the mechanical forces of nature, the intertwining principles of mass and acceleration, or the role of friction. But I had never considered with such urgency the power of true bullets, nor had my limited imagination envisioned pools of blood on fallen cherry blossoms. I was frightened that my friend might die; and yet, a strange exhilaration coursed like lightning through me as I wondered whose blood would be spilled today.

After I had followed him for a mile through the woods, we came to a clearing where the creek and river joined. A small grassy field, perhaps twenty yards on each side, had been selected as the site of the duel. Our adversaries had not yet arrived, so Razor leaned against a tree, cupped both hands in front of his mouth and lit a cigarette. After a couple of puffs, he removed a bag of M&M chocolates from his pocket. "I bet Tom never told you about the time we stole the canister of nitrous from Doctor Bentley's office, got an ounce of pot, a case of beer, and took Belinda and Jane water skiing." His tone was light and airy. "You should have seen us. Your goddam brother was so juiced up he almost flipped the damn boat. But the best was when we roared through the 'No Wake' zone near the Country Club and Belinda mooned those bastards on the dock. You should have seen them. Their stupid mouths opened so wide you could see clear down to their assholes. Naturally, when the Coast Guard finally tailed in on us, we had to ditch the nitrous and the pot in the river. I always regretted that. It was damn good pot." He crushed out his cigarette and then went on much more seriously. "Listen Ace, if anything happens to me, you just get your ass out of here. No one knows who you are and the only reason I asked you was so I'd have a proper second and the damn fool couldn't bitch about improper appearances. So you just beat it, OK? Everything will work itself out." I nodded, knowing he was lying, but incredibly touched that perhaps his last earthly concern should be my welfare.

He abruptly stopped talking as we heard the approach of footsteps. Two men in military dress emerged from another path that led to the clearing. In the lead was a pale, thin man in his fifties who stood stiffly erect. His graying hair was trimmed close to his boxlike skull, and his expression was very somber, like that of a priest about to perform at Mass. His companion was of lesser rank, or so I guessed, as he had fewer ribbons and less fancy epaulets upon his shoulders. His lower face had a twitch on one side that was accentuated by his nervous excitement. They both wore immaculate white gloves and the junior officer carried a beautifully polished mahogany case. When we converged in the center of the field, the Colonel began to speak most solemnly. "Mr. Roundtree, this is my second Lieutenant Waverly."

The two men nodded, and then Razor spoke. "Colonel McCarty, Lieutenant Waverly. This is my second, Doctor Belkin." I fought hard to suppress a grin as I nodded at the men. Even as the gates of the next world rose before him, Razor was conferring honorary degrees.

The Lieutenant spoke quietly to his superior officer, "Colonel, please do reconsider this duel. These circumstances, however unpleasant, could be resolved by an act of Christian charity, forgiveness, on your part. Surely it is not necessary that human life be taken." But he spoke so insincerely, so mechanically and calmly, that it was clear he was merely mouthing what he thought a second should say in such cases.

The Colonel stared straight ahead, looking at no one. "Lieutenant Waverly, Mr. Roundtree has forever stained the integrity of my good name. Moreover, he has sullied the dignity of my beloved wife. No honorable man could allow such grave insults to go unavenged." A long awkward pause followed his speech. Perhaps I was supposed to persuade them to stop this charade. Only it was no charade, and I was speechless. I doubt in any case whether an impassioned appeal on my part would have elicited either an apology from Razor or, had one been forthcoming, its acceptance by the Colonel. Someone was to be shot.

The Lieutenant finally spoke, "Well, since nothing remains to be said, let us continue. I have brought the pistols." He raised and opened the mahogany case to reveal a pair of 9mm Browning handguns that lay inside. Each was eight inches long, intricately engraved with rococo flourishes and sported a polished wooden handle. "Mr. Roundtree, choose your weapon."

Razor chose the lower gun and raised it to his eye as if he were performing a ritual. He checked the safety, gauged the weight, inspected the barrel, and finally he loaded the magazine. With grim satisfaction, he pointed the gun over the river and lined up the sights. The Colonel stood opposite him, holding his own weapon. Razor turned to McCarty and gesturing with his gun, he chuckled. "Nice heat, Colonel." The colonel's face grew livid, but he made no reply. Razor's grin grew broader, and he offered the bag of candy to his opponent. "M&M?" he asked. As he trembled in disgust, the Colonel turned and walked away.

The sun was just beginning to peek over the trees and a glossy mist lay suspended atop the river as together Waverly and I marked off the twelve paces. "Smart of Roundtree to bring a doctor. One of the stupid bastards is sure to need one," he whispered as his vicious smile twitched.

I showed Razor to his spot and murmured gently, "There's still time to call this thing off." I felt extremely giddy and lightheaded, as again the gravity of the situation pressed upon me. He winked at me as he shook his head. "Then God be with you," I murmured, which I instantly realized was a strange remark for an atheist to make at such a moment. Razor looked at me, his rogue's eyes beaming, and then he nonchalantly tossed me the bag of chocolates. I have never admired the courage of a man as much as I admired Razor Roundtree's at that moment before the duel. A maple tree stood off to the left and behind my friend and I went to lean against it for support. My weakened heart beat madly in anticipation. It had been decided that as the injured party, the Colonel, would have the first shot and he raised his gun to take aim. Razor still smiled, seemingly unafraid, and popped his single remaining chocolate into his mouth. The Colonel straightened his arm and the crack of a pistol shot resounded through the early morning quiet. As to what followed, I cannot say. For that is precisely when I fainted.

I do not know how long I lay unconscious. The sun had risen high over the riverbank and the mist had evaporated when I awakened in the field. I looked around, still dazed, and realized I was cold and alone. I struggled to sit up, but the pounding in my head was most unbearable; and when I touched the back of my skull I found a sticky lump. I must have hit my head when I fell. I tried to reconstruct the events of the morning as I stumbled about the field. I roughly calculated where each of the duelists had stood. But as I approached the spot where Razor had faced the Colonel, I was suddenly horrified at the sight of a large purple stain that blemished the flattened grass and seeped into the surrounding earth. A straight path of beaten down weeds led away from the spot, as if a body had been dragged from there. I followed the path to the edge of the field, but I found no corpse there. With much trepidation I recrossed the ground and gingerly peered over the riverbank; but again, there was no sign of Razor or the Colonel.

I was so exhausted and confused that I slumped into an amorphous heap upon the grass and waited for some assistance. But soon I realized no one was coming to help me, so I gathered what strength I could and wandered back along the path. This time I paid no attention to the cherry blossoms, the dogwood or the greens of spring. Finally, an hour later, I stumbled breathlessly to my car. As I settled into the front seat, I thought with the sad bemusement of the strange reprieve bestowed upon my physics class; and then I realized how happy I would be just to pet my faithful Newton once again.

I spent the next few days feverishly seeking clues as to what had happened. I read the obituaries, but there was nothing there; nor were there any articles in the "City Section" of the newspaper, where accounts of homicides and mysteriously found bodies are reported. I called the morgue to inquire about unclaimed corpses, but when the coroner became more interested in asking me questions than giving me answers, I hung up the phone. I even called the Military Institute to ask about the Colonel, only to find out that he had taken a leave of absence six months ago, moved away, and no one had heard from him in the interim. I had simply run out of leads, and as I am no Sherlock Holmes, I resolved to let the matter rest.

Neither my brother nor I heard anything of Razor. Often over the years we would gather for family gatherings and inevitably, in the course of the meal a Razor Roundtree story would be told. My brother would always conclude it with laughter, "I wonder what old Razor is doing these days? Who knows what trouble he's into now?" I always kept silent considering possibilities that my brother couldn't. I saw nothing to be gained in revealing what had unfolded on that fateful morning by the river. And there the affair of Razor Roundtree ended.

Seven years passed and I was now an assistant principal at the school. Towards the middle of October, I was dispatched to the state capitol to attend a conference on school discipline. At the conclusion of the first day's meetings, I attended a reception in one of the dreary, overbearing hotel ballrooms, where the layered, dull brown curtains skirt the walls and the cracked crystal chandeliers suffuse the smoky air with their pale yellow glow. While I stood in line at the bar, I found myself face to face with a military man whose appearance evoked an unnamed anxiety within me. I hoped for a clue and I nodded to him. With a blank, polite expression that acknowledged manners but not recognition, he returned the gesture. It was only as he turned away and revealed a telltale facial twitch, that memory spoke his name to consciousness: Waverly.

I pushed through the sodden, doughy crowd to apprehend him, but as I grew near, I saw he was speaking intimately with a lady and I was reluctant to interrupt. I studied her as I debated when to speak to him. She was in her late fifties and had long since faded, with lifeless hair and pinched, brittle skin. Her heavy-lidded eyes, the irregular lines of lipstick on her too gay smile and her not too steady but careful stance suggested a close acquaintance with the bottle. I concluded my appearance could hardly hurt Waverly's standing with her.

"Good evening, I see you're from the Institute. I used to know some men who taught there. My name is Belkin, Arturo Belkin." I extended my hand towards him and watched his eyes for recognition.

He grasped my hand firmly. "Nice to meet you, Belkin. I'm Lieutenant Colonel Waverly, and please allow me to introduce my fiancée, Mrs. McCarty." I shuddered as he spoke the name. The Colonel's second was now engaged to his wife? "Are you alright, Belkin? You look as if you'd... you know, you do look strangely familiar? Have we met before?"

"I was thinking the same thing," I stammered. I couldn't find the words to touch upon the cruel subject in the presence of the Colonel's widow, and what a disappointment she was. Even with a generous accounting for the time since her liaison with young Razor Roundtree, she had clearly never been a beauty. Perhaps over the years I had romanticized her into a charming, docile young creature forced against her will by cruel parents into a marriage with an unforgiving, older husband. But this woman was coarse looking, plain, worse than plain, she was decrepit, a drunk; and I could not believe that two brave men had fought a duel because of her, and even more dismaying, that one of them had died.

Suddenly, the man grew excited. "My God, man, you were the one at the Colonel's duel. You and that Razor Roundtree. Susan, this is the fellow who was Roundtree's second at the duel."

"How charming," she drawled. "That was something special, wasn't it?"

"Charming, yes, and very special," I muttered. "What happened to the Colonel, if I may ask?"

Her smile showed a line of yellow teeth. "Oh, the poor dear died of a heart attack about a year ago, not too long after we returned to the Institute. It took us completely by surprise. He was drilling the cadets on a field near the Japanese steakhouse. Don't you think that sushi leaves something dangerous in the air? I've always been suspicious of those Japanese. They're such short people. And that sweet Razor. What in heaven's name happened to him?"

I looked over to Waverly, who eyed me with curious anticipation. "I couldn't say for sure." I lied to protect Waverly, in case he hadn't told her what her story had just confirmed to me: my old friend Razor was dead.

But the fool chimed in heartily, "Come on, Belkin, make a clean breast of it. Tell us what happened to the man."

"Perhaps you should tell her," I sneered.

"What? How the hell should I know what happened to the bastard. I last saw him with you."

"And I last saw him facing the Colonel's pistol."

"For Christ's sake Belkin, what are you talking about?"

So I explained to this strange couple how I had awakened alone in the blood drenched field, searched unsuccessfully through the woods and across the city for some sign of Razor's or the Colonel's body, and when I found no clues, I had given up all hope of solving the mystery.

The couple erupted in drunken laughter. At length, Waverly caught his breath so he could speak. "And you haven't seen Roundtree since then?" I nodded and they laughed even harder. "Oh, Belkin, what a scoundrel your friend Roundtree was. Leaving you alone like that. What a crowd you must run with!" And they both burst into laughter again.

"Well, what did happen after I passed out?" I asked impatiently. But the irritating laughter continued as streams of mascara lined tears smirched the woman's heavily rouged cheeks.

At last, Waverly told his tale. "To be truthful, my friend, there was quite a scene when you passed out. You see, the Colonel was so furious with Roundtree that the old man couldn't steady his gun. At length the poor fellow had no choice but to fire, and he did so; but just as it became clear his shot had gone wide of the target, you suddenly collapsed next to the tree. Naturally, we believed you had been the victim of his bullet. The three of us converged upon you to find blood spurting out of your head.

"So, the Colonel, Roundtree and I dragged you to the center of the field to get a better look at you. The bleeding persisted there for quite a while, but eventually, with a pressure dressing fashioned out of a jacket, we were able to control it. Only then did we realize you hadn't been shot, but had instead hit your head on a sharp rock when you fell. Well, as you can imagine, when we grasped that you had not been the victim of the Colonel's shaky hand, Rountree and I broke into convulsions of laughter. Not at you," he assured me. "No, we were not laughing at you, my friend, but out of relief that you were safe. Of course. That's why we laughed.

"But the Colonel, oh The Colonel. When he saw the comic turn the proceedings had taken, he became as furious as a northeast wind. And he insisted that we complete the duel, that your friend Roundtree take his shot. Still rolling in laughter, Roundtree naturally refused, pleading he had to care of his fallen comrade. But the Colonel would hear nothing of it. No, that man ruled like a South American dictator. He demanded that Roundtree take his shot. So we left you like one more lump in the grass, marched off the twelve paces and Roundtree fired his pistol. Into the river. I have never seen the Colonel so disgusted and humiliated, but what could he do? Challenge the man to another duel? He grabbed me by the shoulder and yanked me down the same path we had come by. I remember looking back to see Roundtree tending to your wound. I never imagined he could be such an ass as to leave you lying there, or I assure you I would have remained with you myself. What a character! And to think you have never heard from him since."

I thanked the Lieutenant Colonel for his story, but declined their offer to share a drink. I wished he and his intended the greatest happiness, and suddenly exhausted, I retired to my room to rest up for the next day's meetings. As I lay in bed, dazzled more than angry as I drifted towards my sleep, I wondered what indeed had happened to old Razor. For wherever he is, I am sure he is up to no good.

YOU AND RUBYBLADES

Aint no love lost for no poor black boy in this town. Aint no love to be lost. Your Mama worryin more about how she look than how you feel. You standin there bleedin outta both knees from some fall on some playground and her eyes dont let go of her eyes in the mirror. She thirty five playin like she twenty. Your Daddy be proud of you in his own Daddy sort of way, callin you *Son* so's to make you both smile. But he aint round here too much. He out hustlin to get you another sister or two. Mama already got you three older sisters. They all sassy eyed looks. They all smells and dancin, and aint got no time of they own. So what they want with you? And then there be Grandma. Shit. You shouldn't'a said no love, but what kinda love luck is it that she has three girls and they all has three girls and then finally comes you?

Ruben Blades has the same name as some singer but aint nobody call him that. Most peoples calls him Ruber but you call him RubyBlades all the time. He call you Inky or InkMan or Ink cause you be the PacMan champ of the second grade at the Harold B. Washington School. The real Inky be a chewin up ghost on the PacMan screen. You and RubyBlades be walkin to school. You both curled with laughter, laggin down the sidewalk, swingin your school books at each other's heads, but you tickled too much to hit anythin cept maybe a shoulder or the side of a neck.

You pass some lady beatin a broom against a blanket tossed over a clothes line, and you say to RubyBlades, *You goin in today?*

I aint decided yet. How bout you?

You figure since you be ten they gonna put you in third grade next time no matter what you do now. You say, *I aint decided yet neither.*

You get to the corner grocery and you and RubyBlades agree without sayin to walk right on in. That store be full of things. It got cakes and candies and ice cream. They keeps the sodas in the back. The fat man at the register be countin out the school kids. *Only three at a time*, he say, but you and RubyBlades know he aint fool enough to leave no register so you walk on by

116

anyway. Once you out of his reach, you slow down, you squeak the bottoms of your sneaks against his floor. You pass the shiny wrapped soaps, the rows of toothpaste and mouthwash. Your eyes stop on a tube of Old Jeronium Shampoo. Once, when you was five and filthy from two days playin outside, Grandma dragged you to the bath. You was stubborn then too, and you kept on screechin in the tub, tryin to rip your Old Jeroniumed head out from between those old soft hands. She hold on and her voice be risin, sweeter than sweet. Maybe she think she singin in church on Sunday, but she only talkin about Mama. *Just give her time, chil'. One day she be older. She a good girl, but sometime she still tryin to be young. Just give her time, chil', you'll see.* But you can't wait to set no watch on Mama time, no Sister time, no Daddy time, no Grandma time. You only got one time to keep, and you yank your head free.

In the store you gettin bored when you see RubyBlades slip a Campbell's chicken noodle inside his coat. You seen him lift things before, seen his best tongue waggin grin, but now what you see be Mr. Register Man raisin a fist as thick as a ham.

Hey you skinny little bastards.

You and RubyBlades takeoff. At the end of the aisle RubyBlades turn right, you turn left. You circle around past the PacMan machine which you tap for good luck, then you see Mr. Register Man be doublin back down the middle aisle. You cut a pivot that would please even Willie G., tap PacMan one more time, then scoot past the aisle where he still chasin you, but now his face be drippin with sweat beads, and he yellin more than he runnin. You catch up to RubyBlades at the cold cuts counter and you both slip behind. The old lady slicin meats there be shakin her head. She dont even think of tryin to stop you. She just keep doin her slicin. You push open the back screen she closed to keep out the flies, and when that screen door slam shut, you find yourself free in the alley. Now you and RubyBlades runnin and laughin again.

Soon you slow your feet down. You say, *What's the chicken noodle shit? They has Spaghettios just down the aisle.*

I like the label. That ok with you?

Then you turn and see Mr. Register Man huffin down the alley. He got both ham fists churnin and he look all crazy in the eyes. He got to be to leave that register. Suddenly your legs understand the true meanin of findin your ass in a sling.

Now you not runnin no more, you be flyin. You be a low swoopin bird. You got prettier wings than Michael J.

Flyin right beside you, RubyBlades spit out *Shit*. Your wings wont raise you out of no dead end alley. The chicken noodle clank against the street, but you aint surprised that aint payment enough, and those ham fists still comes chasin you down. Your mind eyes sees his crazy face lit with fire, but your real eyes be good, and when they sees the open door your feets shouts up, yes yes, up, and RubyBlades be just behind you.

You jump up the ramp, movin too fast to think a ramp be somethin strange here, and you inside the door. The room be a hallway and cept for one shaded light at the end, it seem awfully dark. The walls be all covered with a saggin, rich lookin cloth, and you smell somethin strong, somethin lemon sweet you know aint nothin real. Then your nose uncover another smell pokin out from underneath. You suck in a deep breath and you know.

You inside Earl Miller's. You seein your Daddy with a red demon face. His arms be shakin, he barely able to hold back his fists, and he shoutin down at you, *You do that one more time and Earl Miller be gettin a special delivery.* You aint never been in no funeral home before, never even thought about one cept as Earl Miller's at the end of Daddy's fist, and you stop right where you be. You aint goin no further even if Mr. Register Man do follow you in, but RubyBlades has slammed the door shut and the fat man dont even knock.

So you and RubyBlades lean real quiet against the thick cloth, waitin to see who goin to chase after you now. Your heart beatin fast and your chest stingin deep, but you pretty good at hidin in the shadows. Aint nobody goin to find Ink in this light.

After a time you catch your breath and whisper, *You think anyone here?*
If they was, they'd be here by now.
How you know that?
And RubyBlades pause first and then he say, *I been here before.*
And you remember Tyrone, RubyBlades' older brother who got hisself shot across the street from the clinic. You whisper, *Let's get outa here.*
No, man. Let's check it out first.
What for? Earl Miller aint hidin no chicken noodles here.
I think you scared, Ink. Yeah, I think you scared cause they brings dead peoples here. Then he go, *Sniff sniff. I think somebody shit his pants cause he in a place full of dead peoples.*
If you smellin shit you best check your own pants cause I aint got none in mine.
You wait a minute then you ask, *What you wanna see here?*
I wanna see who be dead.

118

You thinkin there aint no good reason to start meetin dead peoples, but you follow RubyBlades down the hall. He go into this room and he stop there. You both see the coffin, all fancy draped with the lid up. There be all sorts of flowered vases and twisted flickery candles surroundin it and then that smell again tickle your nose and you get suspicious of everythin, of RubyBlades, the flowers, the twisted flickery candlelights. But RubyBlades go struttin between the rows of foldin chairs right on up to the dead person.

You catch up, promisin to who listenin that you'll never make Grandma mad again. You'll stop punchin your sisters. You wont skip school so much. You follow him up to the coffin, take a deep breath and peak over the edge.

You surprised to see Mr. Trusty. He laid out like he be nappin, his folded hands restin on a nice full belly, but you know aint nobody really sleep that way. He used to sit in his beach chair near the corner, listenin to his radio, wavin hello with the walkin cane he kept settled on his lap. He wave hello to everybody. Now he seem a little puffed out and waxy, but he don't look too unhappy.

You feel all swolled up inside, real hot and real cold mixed up together. Then you see RubyBlades. His shoulders be shakin, his eyes drippin tears. You never seen him this way before and you surprised he so upset Mr. Trusty be dead. Then you hear him croak out, *Tyrone.*

Tyrone.

You think how many times you gone to bed wishin your sisters be your brothers. You think of Grandma's rheumatism, of her pressure pills she dont take. You lay your arm across his shoulder the way your Daddy sometime do to you. You pull RubyBlades away from dead Mr. Trusty. RubyBlades wipe his sleeve across his nose, and you say, *Let's go find my Grandma. That woman make one mean baloney sandwich.*

CROSSING THE LINE

I offered to suture one leg while Lou did the other. Juan had been hanging on the corner with his buddies when some neighborhood bullies came up the street. It turned out that Juan's friends were faster than he was, and he was tossed, legs first, through a bodega's plate glass window. The shattered glass left a crisscross of wounds that ran from his shins to his thighs. Lou said, "No. I'll sew them myself. If I needed help, I would've called a surgeon. You should eat while things are quiet. I'll never hear the end of it if you miss dinner."

"It won't take long if we both do it."

He shrugged his shoulders and said to the boy, "Juan, Dr. Nelson's going to sew up your other leg."

The boy edged his head off the pillow and peered down over his chin at us. "Just so he knows what he's doing."

"Absolutely. He's a notorious leg man from way back."

I said, "In ten days, Juan, meet us right here in ten days and we'll see which leg looks better." I removed my white jacket and rolled up my shirt sleeves to scrub. After donning mask and gloves I settled onto a stool next to Lou's, and for the next half hour we worked side by side with easy precision. Lou finished first, and after he'd washed, he came over and stood behind me. I leaned away from the wound I was closing to examine the leg in a longer perspective. I figured that's what he was doing: gauging my alignment of torn skin, observing where I'd placed my sutures and how tight the knots were.

He clapped me hard on the shoulder, almost knocking me off the stool. "I'll meet you outside when you're done."

"It's lucky I was between stitches just then."

"There's no luck involved."

When I finished, I passed through the silent emergency room and found Lou in the lobby. He was squatting, pointing to the lip of his shirt pocket while a hesitant girl considered which lollipop she wanted. As usual, he wasn't wearing his white jacket. He believed it scared the children—he didn't care what the parents thought—and when he was the senior resident in charge, his jacket never left the coat rack behind the ER desk. He wore instead open necked shirts with the sleeves rolled up, casually displaying his thick forearms. His wavy brown hair was the color of wet oak leaves, and his pale blue eyes were nearly hidden by drooping lids which concealed his quick, intelligent nature. At last, the girl chose a green one. He rose, and while patting her shoulder, he said something to her mother that ended with the three of them laughing. When he saw me he turned and spread his arms, a gesture meant to engulf the empty lobby and request the tribute due to one who has conjured up a quiet emergency room. "Looks like I'm giving you one more easy night on call."

I pointed through the window at the bright sunlight. "I'd say you're calling it a little early."

"And working Thursday, you have the whole goddam weekend off. What an easy life you lead, Roger."

"Right. My first free weekend in two months. And I'll probably spend it sleeping."

"Or at least in bed. How is Miss Amy, anyway? We haven't seen her for a while."

"Amy's fine. Have you and Diane made any plans?"

"I thought I'd spend Saturday here."

"Great idea. Then you'll have Sunday to rest up."

He was looking at an empty wheelchair parked in a corner. "Typical Roger, always looking at the bright side. I suppose you're coming to dinner tomorrow night?"

"You know I never miss a Friday at Chez Lou et Diane."

"Thank God for small favors."

He was teasing, of course. Otherwise, he and Diane wouldn't have hosted those Friday night dinners for all the pediatric residents who weren't working. Diane refused any offers of help, though she never knew how many of us would be there nor when we would arrive. She might prepare a bubbling pot of chili or a huge bowl of spaghetti topped with homemade tomato sauce and Parmesan cheese. In the winter she would serve platters of roasted vegetables. In the summer she made salads with produce from a local farmers market. She tossed those salads in an amazing dressing created from a secret family recipe she refused to share. And there were always at least two kinds of beer. This Friday night tradition had begun several months before Lou moved into her house, and after awhile it seemed natural that we had gathered under her wing; for among the wives and girlfriends attached to our clan in those days, she was the only one who seemed to appreciate, rather than merely tolerate, our company. I don't know why she was so kind to us. Perhaps it was only that she shared our devotion to children—she taught kindergarten—but for the most part, I think she would have been just as unfettered and nurturing in any group she fell into, that she would have created similar banquets for an ashram of Krishnas or a band of Hell's Angels—using different menus, of course—if chance had brought them to her instead of us.

I heard the phone slam down, and Erica, the head nurse, pushed open the door and hollered, "Blue Taxi's coming in with a baby born at home." Lou opened his mouth but she waved him off. "I told you all I know." Her thick voice tailed away as she stalked back into the emergency room. Silently, Lou and I considered the possibilities: prematurity, cold stress, hypoglycemia. While we waited the baby could be hemorrhaging or slipping into sepsis, and if we were really lucky, the mother would be a junkie.

"It looks like I might miss dinner after all."

"So what's the big deal? You'll just eat more tomorrow."

We heard an approaching siren, and a blue police car, its cherrytop spinning, swerved into the drive. Officer Fitzpatrick was behind the wheel. Fitz was a regular on this circuit and after he'd swiveled his bulk out of the car, he tipped his hat to us, then supported the elbow of the woman emerging from the back seat shadows. Pale and wobbly, she pressed a swaddled baby close to her chest. Erica pushed between Lou and me, and pried the infant free from the mother's arms. "The doctor will want to check him right away," she said firmly.

Erica rushed away, and the door flapped shut behind her. She didn't hear the soft reply, "She's a girl."

I held the door for Fitz and the mother, then led them back to the treatment room. Under a heat lamp Erica and Lou were examining the baby. She was a fair-sized infant, maybe seven pounds, and she waved her tiny fists vigorously. When Erica pricked her heel, squeezing out a drop of blood to check her sugar, the baby screamed a healthy, high-pitched cry. Her mother stood anxiously beside me. Her long, heavy boned face was ringed by matted roots of greasy blonde hair, and her summer frock, which had once been bright yellow, had faded until only traces of color remained here and there, tiny islands surrounded by a sweat soaked, gray sea.

"Please sit down. You must be exhausted," I said, leading her to a chair in the corner.

"Isn't she pretty? Isn't she a pretty little girl?"

"She certainly is."

Erica said, "Her D-stick is 80."

Alarmed, the mother jumped up, "What? What's that?"

"It means her blood sugar's fine," Lou replied, removing the stethoscope from his ears. "She looks good, real good. I can't believe how well she's been cleaned and bathed." He touched the infant's belly. "And the umbilical cord looks great. Who did all this?"

"See, my boyfriend and me took this childbirth class. They teach you all that junk there."

"They gave you the triple dye and the clip for the cord?" The mother nodded. "Did you get any drops for her eyes?"

"What?"

"We can do that here," I said.

"And don't forget the Vitamin K."

"Of course." I frowned and shook my head. As if I didn't know to give Vitamin K. Lou saw my irritation and shrugged, dismissing his overbearing compulsion. I turned to the mother. She was rocking back and forth on the chair, her arms wrapped around her stomach, and her large brown eyes were moist, almost glistening, as she stared at her baby. When she felt me watching, she turned and smiled a ragged smile. "Oh, that's a pretty little girl."

I felt touched by her great joy, and a soft deference eased into my voice. "We'd like to keep her for a few days, just to run a few tests and make sure there aren't any problems."

"Whatever you think's best."

Erica twitched her nose at the heap of dirty quilt the infant had arrived in, and swaddled the baby in a hospital blanket. She was settling the child into her mother's arms when Lou nodded towards me and said to the woman, "Oh, don't you worry. Dr. Nelson here is one of the finest. Your baby couldn't be in better hands." And if you hadn't known him well, you would never have detected the playful sarcasm in his voice.

The quiet of the early evening was deceptive. After Lou went home, the pulse of the night quickened, its pressure soared. The gathering faces skipped past me, raced beyond blurring, accelerating until what memory distilled was but a strange montage: the heavy lidded eyes of the toddler who had downed his mother's valium, the flushed cheeks of the boy with diabetic keto-acidosis, the clenched jaw of the Black girl writhing in pain from her sickle cell anemia. Then just before the dawn a fulcrum for the night appeared, a limp infant with a ridge of tiny vertebrae that didn't move, didn't give the slightest shudder, as my spinal needle slid between the peaks; and a few hours later that child was dead from meningitis.

In other words, it was a typical night. I never saw my bed, though I did find a few minutes to call Amy. By then the contours of the night were clearly visible and I was already looking forward to Friday's release.

"No way," she'd said. I had foolishly suggested she join me for dinner at Lou and Diane's. We had been together long enough for her to tell me plainly what she thought of my friends. "It's not that I don't like them. One at a time they're okay—sometimes. But in groups, forget it. All you talk about is the hospital. And that's when you're civilized."

"Jesus, lighten up a bit, will you? We're just letting off some steam."

"Oh I know. This is your band of brothers. You'd take a bullet for any of them. The best friends you ever had."

"That's right. I know they always have my back. This job is tough and I couldn't survive without these guys. They really are my band of brothers. Come on, Amy. These weekend nights are healthy. We need to vent."

"Well, you'll have to vent without me."

"Diane doesn't seem to mind."

"So she's either a fool or a saint. Roger, what can I tell you? I'm pleading sanity. It shouldn't come as news to you that I won't go over there." The last time she'd given in she found herself sharing a love seat with Bill Hall's pet boa constrictor. This was only a week after Bill's frustration had erupted and no one could stop him from painting Jasper's testicles blue. Jasper was Diane's dog.

I said, "So I guess I'll see you Saturday."

"Okay. And good luck tonight. It sounds like you'll need it."

I didn't tell her about the little girl who was born at home. By the time I'd hung up the phone, that child had been sleeping quietly for hours. More urgent matters crowded her out of consciousness until the next morning, when one of my interns said the police wanted to see me. Immediately, I thought of the infant who had arrived in Fitz's blue taxi, and sure enough, when I entered the corridor Fitz was waiting there for me. Standing beside him was a reedy, sallow faced man wearing the standard Eliot Ness hat and brown shoes. He shifted his weight impatiently from leg to leg. My guess was he was Fitz's Lieutenant, but I was wrong. He introduced himself as Special Agent Schomer, FBI.

"You saw that baby he brought in yesterday?" He jerked his thumb towards Fitz.

"Sure. What's this about?"

He ignored my question. "How old was the baby when you first saw her?"

"I couldn't say exactly."

"A few hours? A few days? A few weeks? C'mon Doc, you are a pediatrician, aren't you?" His foot tapped a few quick beats.

"Yes," I answered, too weary to be angry. "I'm definitely a pediatrician. And the baby was definitely born yesterday. If that's close enough for you."

"That's fine. Yes, that's just fine." The FBI man nodded to Fitzpatrick, then asked me, "Do you know where we might find the mother?"

"No, but we can see if she's with the baby."

We found her rocking the child in a corner of the nursery. Her face was bowed over the infant's head and she was singing to her softly. As Schomer introduced himself I saw that beneath the white hospital gown she was wearing the same clothes she'd worn yesterday. When he asked me if there was a room where they could speak privately, the woman and I shared a look of questioning eyes, but she said nothing. I offered him the office in the back. She straightened the baby's blanket, kissed her on each cheek, then settled her into the crib. Schomer was all patience now. There was no more foot tapping or weight shifting, and when she was ready, he escorted her to the office and closed the door.

After they'd been inside a few minutes I asked Fitzpatrick, "What's this was all about?"

He hesitated, rubbing his tough, square chin before he said, "Well, we're not so sure it's her baby."

"What?"

"There was a newborn kidnapped from the nursery at City General yesterday. I heard the report on the radio just as I'm leaving here, so I started thinking...and it's always best to report, just in case, you see. So I'm talking to Tom Pagani, he's the desk sergeant back at the station house, and he says to me, he says, 'Fitz, who knows? Maybe, you're onto something.' So he calls the

FBI, and they send us this Special Agent Schomer, and I can tell you one thing—just from listening to the man talk all morning—if that's the baby we're looking for, you can be sure every bit of credit's going to the FBI and not a drop to us fellas in blue."

Just then the office door opened. The young woman emerged in front, her wrists in handcuffs. Her tear streaked face hung slack. Fitz hurried over, and flanked by the officers, the woman crossed the suddenly quiet nursery. She kept her eyes lowered until she reached the entrance, and then she stopped and turned and stared at the crib. Schomer waited a few seconds before gently pulling on her arm. She offered no resistance but as she passed through the door she unleashed a sob, a wailing so pitiful I felt the hairs on the back of my neck rise, and her anguish swelled to fill the hallway, the tiny office, and even the nursery itself, until she reached the end of the corridor and was swallowed up by the closing of the elevator doors.

On Friday night I arrived at Diane's house an hour before sunset. She lived in an old mansion with a squeaky, front porch swing. The property belonged to her father, a successful real estate developer who had retreated to the suburbs long ago. I assumed he helped support her—how else could she afford all that food—and he let her stay in the house while his company acquired the surrounding land. She said when he owned the entire block he planned to replace the mansion and surrounding row houses with a granite faced tower of condominiums, but Diane had settled in as if that day would never come. Of course, her living space was confined to the first floor, as her father had refused to rehab the upstairs beyond the bare minimum. Her living room had a sofa and a couple of club chairs covered with the same red and white floral print. Against one wall was a polished, walnut hutch and matching sideboard which had been passed down from her grandmother, and in a corner, a cushioned wicker pod was suspended from the ceiling. Lou had been going out with Diane for over a year when he moved in, and since I was his closest friend among the residents, I accepted his request to help with the move. It was an easy favor as it had required only one trip in each of our cars. We'd packed his clothes and weights into his Saab, while the stereo, records, and medical books filled the back of my Datsun. It surprised me that after only a few weeks, it was easy to see how the house had changed. For one thing, it was cleaner; and though he didn't have much, Lou had clearly left his signature. His stereo had replaced her old boombox in the living room, and his weights now occupied a corner of the dining room. Back issues of *Cosmopolitan* mingled with *The Journal of Pediatrics* on the coffee table top.

When I pulled into the driveway, Bill Hall was stretched out on the porch, his elbows propped against the steps. Two beers were standing guard beside him.

"Is one of those Janie's?"

He shook his ragged mop of hair. "Nah, they're both mine. I'm trying to cut back on my trips to the kitchen."

"I understand—you'd only be in the way in there."

"Roger, Roger."

I grimaced at the old joke. In the kitchen Bill's current flame, Janie, was molding hamburger patties. Diane was arranging bowls of coleslaw and potato salad around a mound of rolls which served as the centerpiece in the bottom of a child's red wagon. She hugged me as if it had been years rather than days since we'd last seen each other. Her delicate features were framed by a frizzy mist of chestnut hair, and her face would've been truly beautiful except for her eyes. They were an attractive shade of green, but when she was tired or had been drinking, the left one turned in, making it difficult to know where to look when she talked to you. She said, "I thought we'd eat at the park. Now that it's Fall, we won't have too many more nights like this."

"That's a sad thought, but where's the master of the house?" Our shoulders rubbed as I reached around her for a beer.

"You mean Lou? He's out buying charcoal and lighter fluid. He'll meet us there."

From the house the four of us meandered down the street to an unlit, and therefore unoccupied, baseball field. I pulled the wagon loaded with food while Bill, stocky and broad shouldered, hefted a large cooler full of beer. Jasper ran in front then circled around and scampered between us. He was a gangly mutt with a short-haired coat resembling a white carpet ruined by coffee stains. When we reached the park Lou was squatting over a hibachi on the pitcher's mound and lighting a fire. We unpacked the wagon, opened some beers, and I lay back on the dying infield grass. Exhausted yet not sleepy, I watched the wispy orange clouds feathering the early evening sky. Jasper loped around the base paths, from third to second to first, raising a leg every few yards to squirt the brown dust.

Diane asked, "Why's he do that? Why doesn't he just pick one spot and let it all go?"

Lou sat Indian style, grilling the burgers, his watch on the ground beside him timing how long each one cooked. "He's leaving his scent, marking out his territory so any other dogs will know it's his."

Bill said, "You sure the sucker just doesn't know how to run the bases?"

"No, Jasper's a fan. He knows the score."

We ate in a circle on the infield grass, eating as if it were our first meal since last Friday's gathering, and in some ways perhaps it was. We knew no one would be called away, that our shared fatigue was safe from sudden challenge. Tonight we would see no one die, and this truce was enough for me. Above us the sky drained from purple to deep blue to black and my eyes were drawn down from the stars to the orange coals winking in the fire.

While we were eating dessert, a blueberry pie topped with vanilla ice cream, Janie slipped on a jacket to ward off the chill. She said, "You guys finally made the big time. Your stolen baby was the headline story on 'Action News' tonight."

Lou asked, "Did they say why she did it?"

"They said she took the baby to give it to her boyfriend. It was supposed to be a present."

"So why'd she bring it to us?"

"Well supposedly, and this is just supposedly now, the boyfriend said it wouldn't be theirs without a birth certificate. So they decided she should take the baby to the hospital to get one."

Bill was incredulous. "Oh Janie, that's crazy."

"I'm just telling you what they said. I didn't say it made any sense."

"A goddam bus wasn't good enough for her? She had to call the police to give her a ride? Too fuckin' much. That's just too fuckin' much." He turned to Lou, "So Sherlock, how come you couldn't figure it out? I mean only a moron would miss a perfectly clipped cord painted with triple dye."

Lou poked the fire and tiny sparks stirred above the coals. "Well, she said she'd taken that class."

"Oh yeah, 'That class.'"

"Well, a class is a class."

Diane said thoughtfully, "She must really love her boyfriend to do something like that."

Bill threw a piece of hamburger roll onto the fire. "We're talking zero synapses here. I mean minimal CNS function. Calling the police after you've kidnapped a baby?"

"And she must've been scared, really scared, but she went through with it anyway."

The irritation crackled in Lou's voice. "Diane, the woman stole a stranger's baby. There are certain things people just don't do. Murder, kidnapping, rape—"

"—And don't forget stuff like mixing 7-Up with Chivas Regal, or giving your grandmother a subscription to Penthouse, or farting at a White House reception." Bill turned to me, "You should never fart at a White House reception."

Lou frowned, "Like I said, there are certain things people just don't do. And she crossed over that line. There's no way you can justify what she did."

Diane said, "I'm not trying to justify anything."

"That's good."

Lou stood up, dusted the front of his pants, then whistled for Jasper. The dog appeared out of the darkness and Lou scratched him behind the ears. "Come on boy. You're the only one here who makes any sense." He grabbed a Frisbee off the wagon and they trotted towards the outfield.

Bill laughed and lit a joint. "He's just pissed he wasn't the one to figure it out. He blew his chance to make the news and it's killing him."

I said, "You're such a sweetheart. But I was there too, and really, as weird as her story was, you have to admit the truth was even stranger."

"Hopeless," he muttered. "Both of you—hopeless." He inhaled deeply from the joint then offered it to me. I shook my head and he passed it to Diane.

I asked her, "And what were you trying to say, if you weren't trying to defend her?"

"I was just trying to imagine it from her side. I was thinking how much she must love her boyfriend that she would do something so horrible just to please him. It must take a special kind of love to make you take that kind of chance. I was just thinking that, in its own way, what she did showed a certain courage."

Bill exhaled a cloud of smoke. "Maybe she was too dumb to be scared."

"Well maybe, but she fooled Lou and Roger and the police."

"And we know how much brains that takes."

A phosphorescent platter spun across the outfield sky and we heard the thudding rush of Jasper giving chase. Suddenly he sprang and clamped his jaws around the Frisbee. "Alright," Lou shouted triumphantly. "I told you he could do it. Good dog. Let's do it again. Attaboy." The glowing Frisbee carved another arc across the night.

Diane giggled, "I've had that dog for three years and could hardly teach him to pee outside."

Bill snuffed out the joint. "That's great. Now they're both ready for the circus. C'mon Janie, they're having too much fun. Let's go bother them." Rejuvenated by the grass, Bill and Janie stumbled towards the dog. They stole the Frisbee and threw it to one another, keeping it from Jasper until he howled in frustration. Their shouts and cheers drifted in from the outfield. I stretched out on my back and smiled at their pleasure. Happy and luxuriating in my fatigue, I made a pillow of my hands and shut my eyes. I listened to their laughter, to the last of the crickets chirping behind the batter's cage, to the squawk of a passing car radio. I wasn't thinking about anything. A blade of grass rubbed my cheek and I pushed it away. A moment later it brushed me again, and this time I swatted clumsily, provoking Diane's close laughter.

"Did I wake you?" She was kneeling beside me, holding the offending blade so I could see it.

"No, just resting." I rolled onto my side. In the dark I couldn't see her eyes.

"You were busy last night?"

"No more than usual. No sleep, twelve admissions, one death."

"I don't know how you handle that."

"Well twelve is a lot. Usually, it's only five or six."

"That's not what I meant."

"I know." I watched the Frisbee fly beyond Jasper's reach.

She paused for a second and then she said, "Amy doesn't like me very much, does she?"

"No. Yes. I mean she does like you. Why would you say that?"

"She never joins us on Friday night."

"Oh, that's not you. That's us. She gets bored hearing us talk about the hospital all the time."

"Not me. What you guys do is amazing. Really."

"Aw shucks, Diane."

"But it's never enough, is it? It's never enough." She shook her head sadly, but I started laughing. She asked, "What's so funny?"

"I just flashed on this time when I was in college. My friend Dave and I went to Vermont one summer to visit my brother. My brother was a hippy dippy guy and he and some friends had rented a small farm with a pond and some woods. Real pretty piece of land. So, Dave and I go visit and my brother has some acid which Dave can't wait to try. Dave and I are tripping and we have all this energy. It's about three in the morning now, everyone else has gone to bed, and we go for a walk through the woods and end up at the pond. It's beautiful. There's a bright full moon shining on the water. It's lighting up the trees. It's just beautiful. We're lost in our trippy thoughts and Dave says to me, 'Why are we here?' And I don't understand the fucking question. Does he mean why are we by the pond? Why are we in Vermont visiting my brother? Why do we exist in the Universe? I just have no fucking idea. Just then, a small light goes streaking across the sky, and I go, 'Hey man, look at that star.' And Dave says, 'Man, that's no star. That's a satellite.'"

"And?"

"And then we both laughed hysterically."

Diane and I laughed as Lou sat down and put his arm around her. She nuzzled her head against his shoulder, and asked me, "Don't we make a great couple?"

"Lovely, absolutely lover-ly."

She turned to Lou, "Is Roger always this sarcastic?"

I said, "I'm serious. All my friends deserve a woman like you." Lou shrugged his shoulders.

"Yes, they look so-oo sweet," Bill crooned, tossing the Frisbee at Lou's head. He looked at me sprawled upon the grass. "Roger, are we going to have to carry you home?"

"Just roll me in the wagon." Jasper loped over and licked my face.

Diane said, "Well, it is getting late and Lou, you do have to work tomorrow."

"As if I could forget. Oh well, I suppose we should put out the fire."

Janie complained, "Not this again."

"Yes," Bill announced, "It's macho ritual time."

Janie turned to Diane. "Why can't they act mature and drink a light beer or something?"

Lou, Bill and I ignored her and picked up the hibachi by the handles. We made our way to a gully we'd found earlier that summer just beyond the left field fence. After we'd dumped the coals into a pile there, Bill said, "Gentlemen, start your zippers—and remember, we only have one chance." We released our streams and the coals fizzled. The acrid scent of urine filled the air. Bill sniffed noisily then exhaled—"Ahhh"—and the three of us chuckled softly. From the distance behind us came the soft peals of Diane's laughter. When we had recrossed the field, we set the hibachi and empty cooler on the wagon. Lou tied a knot in the top of the trash bag and looped it around Jasper's collar. The sweet evening air blew cool, Jasper's collar jingled and the wagon wheels squeaked as our ragged parade returned to Diane's house.

I wasn't the first one to spend a Friday night on a couch at Diane's house. I don't remember much of what happened after we arrived, though I know I was once awakened by music and later, or at least I think it was later, by Jasper's howling. That time I saw Bill grinning and waving a can of paint as he chased the dog around a coffee table. I fell asleep as he stopped and said, "Aww Janie, I was only testing his memory. I wasn't gonna do anything."

When I awakened it was light outside. The house was quiet, and a soft breeze rippled through the curtains above me. I rearranged the blanket on the sofa and reveled in the rebirth I felt in my head and limbs after a good night's sleep. A few minutes later I stretched and opened my eyes. In the bedroom Diane stood before a mirror, running a brush through her hair. She was naked except for her red panties, and stunned I stared at the taut valentine until finally she turned around and caught me. I took a guilty deep breath. Her face remained neutral, betraying nothing, and she kept her eyes locked on mine as she walked slowly to the door. She stopped there, leaned against the doorjamb and then she smiled. I had never seen such sultry eyes. I didn't move. I didn't speak. She stood there for a long minute, then pursed her lips as she casually slipped her thumbs to inch lower the waistband of her panties. "What's the matter? Do you need an engraved invitation?"

The light glittered in her eyes, danced in streaks along the chestnut hair that curled down to her shoulders. "A-as a matter of fact, I don't."

When we finished our residencies, we scattered. Bill joined an HMO outside of Phoenix. Three from our group converted an abandoned church in Camden into a clinic for the poor. Eventually I married Amy and I hung my shingle in her hometown—Pawtucket, Rhode Island. On the last Christmas Eve we would spend as residents, Lou moved out of Diane's house. He never told me why and I was not inclined to ask. Several months later he landed a job with a well-heeled practice in a Chicago suburb. They were busy and he did well, learning quickly that discerning parents believe the best pediatricians wear a tie and starched white jacket. His wardrobe grew. We kept in touch—a phone call every month or two, a card at Christmas—and every summer after attending a conference on the Cape, he'd take a couple of days to visit Amy and me. When I last saw him the three of us went to a nearby state park for a picnic. Amy, seven months pregnant with our first child, was easily tired in the August heat and she spent most of the day propped against the trunk of a shady maple. Lou and I were too restless to only talk all afternoon and we decided to take a swim in the lake. We started off vigorously, pushing easily through the cool, placid water until we were well past the canoes and sailboats skirting the shoreline. We reached an unspoken agreement to continue to the far beach, but as we neared the halfway point I knew I didn't have enough wind to swim that far and back, so I stopped and began to tread water. He swam on for a minute, then turned around. I was facing the shore, and when Amy saw me looking she waved.

"I envy you," he said.

"Why?"

"You and Amy seem so happy."

I wasn't sure if we were happy or not, but I knew I didn't want to have that conversation with him. I said, "But what about you? All those luscious midwestern girls must be dying for a piece of a good looking, young doctor. All those girls—"

"No. It's not like you think." He dipped his head beneath the surface, then popped up and sprayed a stream of water through the air. "Do you ever hear from Diane? Is she still married to that dentist?"

"As far as I know."

He waited until our eyes met. "You know, I've thought about this, thought about it a lot actually, and I think I made a mistake when I left her. We should've gotten married. She really loved me, you know. She really did."

I imagined the Diane he was remembering, and if I were Lou I might have missed her, too. But when I recalled my September valentine, I imagined a darker marriage, full of secrets, a marriage where anger dissipated into apathy. What if I were to tell him about that morning and all the others that followed when I joined Diane in her bed just after he had left for call? What if he were to suddenly see that Diane, the Diane who had beckoned me from the doorway? Would he understand his memories were deceiving him? Maybe my few words could relieve his deep, yet misplaced, longing. And I wouldn't have to tell him the truth. Though I had never felt any strong guilt about our affair, it would be easy enough to say it was Bill Hall or someone else that she had summoned from the couch. (And hadn't I wondered about that also?) But what seemed most likely was that anything I said, regardless of its truth, would only raise his anger or call out his pain. Sometimes the best of our poor gifts is silence.

A breeze had come up and some sailboats whisked away from the pack of canoes. Some novice sailors attempted to turn and tack towards the dock, but most of the skiffs caught the wind and sailed with it, slicing a path between the waves that separated Lou and me from the beach. We were watching them, still treading water, and I said to him, "Marry Diane? Don't be ridiculous. She was only after your money. C'mon, I'll race you to the shore."

ABOUT THE AUTHOR

Steve Levin grew up in Newport News, Virginia. He graduated from Duke University and received his MD from Virginia Commonwealth University. For 33 years he practiced pediatrics in Camden and Philadelphia. He currently resides with his wife in Philadelphia. He collaborated with author Bruce E. Field on *As Always: The Letters of Pickles and Zorro,* a collection of their correspondence. This is his first book of fiction.

www.ingramcontent.com/pod-product-compliance
Lightning Source LLC
Chambersburg PA
CBHW060231180626
46813CB00007B/3042